TIM BOWLER

NIGHT RUNNER

OXFORD
UNIVERSITY PRESS

OXFORD
UNIVERSITY PRESS

Great Clarendon Street, Oxford OX2 6DP
Oxford University Press is a department of the University of Oxford.
It furthers the University's objective of excellence in research, scholarship,
and education by publishing worldwide. Oxford is a registered trade mark of
Oxford University Press in the UK and in certain other countries

British Library Cataloguing in Publication Data

Data available

ISBN: 978-0-19-279414-7

1 3 5 7 9 10 8 6 4 2

Printed in Great Britain

Paper used in the production of this book is a natural,
recyclable product made from wood grown in sustainable forests.
The manufacturing process conforms to the environmental
regulations of the country of origin.

FOR MY FATHER, WITH LOVE

CHAPTER 1

There's no other way to put this: I've had it up to here.
If it's not Dad whipping off his belt, it's Mum snapping
at me like she never used to, or the bullyboys hunting
me at school, or the headmaster asking me if I've got
any friends when he bloody knows I haven't. I've even
had the landlord saying Zinny's not a proper name for a
fifteen-year-old boy and how come my parents can buy
me new running shoes when they never pay the rent on
time? And now there's a guy in the street watching my
window.

Don't know who he is, just know he looks normal
and feels wrong. I mean, what's he doing down the slug
end of the road anyway? Just dingy old houses. What's
to look at? I keep to the side of the window and go on
peeking round the curtain. Big guy, about thirty, neat
hair, clean shaven. Not short of money with a flash coat
like that. I caught sight of him a few minutes ago walking down the opposite pavement.

Nothing wrong with that. Not everyone thinks Abbot
Street's a cesspit. Some people even live here. But down
this end? He's gone past the shops and most of the other

houses and now he's stopped, and he's still staring up at my window. Doesn't look like someone the school's sent to find me. He's heading for the front door. I step back from the window. There's a knock down below.

'We've got a bell,' I murmur.

It rings, rings again, then silence falls: just the sound of traffic from the main road, then that seems to fade, and all I hear is a blackbird chirping up on the roof. Feels strange for a few seconds, like the city's turned into a country meadow. Not that I've ever been in one. The bell rings again.

I sit on the bed and wait. He's got to give up soon. I want to go back to the window and check round the curtain again, but I don't dare. I've got a feeling he might look up and catch me. I think of Mum and Dad. Maybe one of them knows him. I hope not. Don't know why. Still the silence. I picture the country meadow again. I often do this. When I can't take the city any more, I think of the nature pictures in that book I've got.

Sound of footsteps outside, moving back from the door. I'm guessing he's looking up at the window again. Then another sound, and this time I relax. He's walking away, not up the road but past the house towards the railway bridge. I jump back to the window and check round the curtains. But I'm too late. There's no sign of him.

He must have moved dead fast. I slip to the other side of the window to give me a better angle. Still no sign, just the street and the bridge and a train clunking over it towards the city centre. I sit back on the bed again and try to think. There's nothing says this guy's trouble, nothing more than my instinct, and that could be wrong. I'm always jumpy when I bunk off school. Then I hear the sound at the back door.

I stiffen. All's quiet again, and for a moment I think I've imagined it, but then it comes back, clear as the thumping of my heart: a scrape, a rattle, another scrape. Someone's trying to pick the lock. A click as it surrenders and the door opens with a creak. I look quickly round. No time to get down the stairs and out the front door, no point running into Mum and Dad's room, or into the bathroom. He'll hear me moving and the only advantage I've got is him not knowing I'm in the house.

If that's true. Best to stay here anyway and hide under the bed. He might just miss me. There's nothing to steal in my room. He'll see that at a glance. He'll see it everywhere else too. Everything about this house'll tell him how poor we are, so with any luck he won't hang around. He's through the kitchen now and into the front room. I can hear him moving about. I kneel down, soft as I can, and check under the bed. Games kit still stuffed under there from last week, plus my old tatty cushion and my running shoes. I wait, listening.

It's gone quiet downstairs and I'm terrified he's heard me, but then the sounds start again. He's pulling open the drawers of the old cabinet. I squeeze under the bed, ease myself towards the middle. Smells musty and I'm worried I'm going to sneeze. I've started trembling too. The unwashed kit's close to my face and it stinks. I pull some of it out of the bag and stuff it down the other side of my body with the cushion.

Don't know why I'm bothering. If he looks under the

bed, he'll see me, with or without this stuff. I curl up, try to make myself small. Sound of footsteps on the stairs. I try to stop trembling, but I can't. He stops outside my door, like he's thinking which room to try first—then he heads for Mum and Dad's. Takes his time in there but I can hear what he's doing.

He's opening all the drawers, tipping stuff out, poking through, and now he's pulling back the wardrobe and the old chest, like he wants to look behind them; then I catch another sound. Can't work it out straightaway, then I get it. He's dragging back the bed, pulling up the carpet and the floorboards. That's when I move, because he'll be in here next, doing the same thing, and I've only got one chance to run.

I crawl out and stand up, praying he hasn't heard me, but it's no good. All the sounds have stopped in Mum and Dad's room. I brace myself. He's listening. He's got to be. He's heard something—me obviously—and any moment now he's going to rush in and see me. But instead he runs down the stairs and out the back door. A crash of the gate and he's off down the alley, his steps clattering away into silence. Then I hear the key in the front door.

And Mum's voice.

CHAPTER 2

'Hello?' she calls.

I don't answer. There's something else wrong now and I don't mean me being here. I mean Mum being here. It's two in the afternoon. She's supposed to be cleaning offices till six. So she said. She calls out again.

'Hello?'

Then a man's voice.

'Take it easy, Dana. There's nobody here.'

I don't recognize the speaker. Don't like him either, now I've guessed what he's come for. It's gone quiet downstairs and I know why. I want to run down and break them up, but I know I've got to keep out of sight. I slip under the bed again and wait for the shout. Nothing for ages. Jesus, they must be glued together. Then footsteps heading for the front room, and Mum's voice.

'Bloody hell!'

'Back door's open,' says the man. 'Could mean they've gone.'

'Or they didn't close it on their way in,' says Mum.

They mutter something I don't hear, then there's more footsteps, this time on the stairs. They're both coming up. I curl up under the bed and peer towards the door. Two pairs of feet stop on the threshold.

'Zinny's room doesn't look any different,' says Mum.

I study Romeo's shoes. They're not smart like the ones the other guy was wearing. They're cheap shit trying to be posh. I feel a sudden urge to crawl out and gob in the man's face. But he's moved away now and Mum's gone with him. I wait again.

'Christ!' says Mum.

They've seen the main bedroom.

'I'm phoning the police,' she says.

'Dana, listen—'

'I'm not going to mention you. You'd better go. Use the back door.'

'It's just that—'

'I told you,' she says. 'I'm not going to mention you. You weren't here, all right?'

'I love you.'

'No, you don't. Now piss off.'

He doesn't, the bastard. There's another silence, then a scuffling sound like she's pushed him away, and then footsteps—his footsteps—heading down the stairs. I picture those shoes again and I'm glad when I hear the back door close and it's all quiet. Except for Mum's voice on the phone.

'Mrs Dana Okoro, that's right, forty-seven Abbot Street.'

Now I've got to risk it. I can't face Mum and the police at the same time. I'm still hoping I can get out without her seeing me. If she tells Dad I was here, it's a belt job this evening. Unless I threaten her with what I know. Can't make up my mind about that. I crawl out again from under the bed and creep over to the door.

Mum's still talking on the phone and she's taken it into the front room. I won't get a better chance than this. I tiptoe down the stairs. The door to the front room's open and I can see her in there. She's got her back to me, one hand holding the phone, the other straightening her hair.

I slip past and head for the kitchen, and she's talking on, like she hasn't heard me, and here's the back door—and shit! I forgot. Romeo closed it on his way out. No way I can open it quietly. It's a noisy beast at the best of times. Then I realize the talking's stopped. I freeze and listen, then Mum speaks again.

'I think there's someone in the house.'

I yank open the door, slam it after me and race off down the path. Through the gate and out into the alley, and I'm pelting as fast as I can towards the railway bridge. I stay low to make sure the wall cuts me off from the house, but I'm pretty sure Mum can't see me. She'd have to run upstairs and get to a window and I think I'm ahead of her. Unless she saw me as I scooted down the path.

I'm out in the street now and cutting over to the railway bridge. Under that and down Hendon Street towards the roundabout, quick stop to catch my breath, then on again, jogging now, past the park and on towards the waste ground. But I can't hide yet. There's something I've got to do first.

Phone box.

No idea how I'm going to do this—I'm rubbish at funny voices—but I've got to try. Mum'll show the police what's happened but she can't tell them anything about the guy who broke in, and I can. I pick up the phone: nine, nine, nine. It rings, then there's a click and a woman asks me which service I want. Only now I can't speak.

'Hello?' she says.

I stare round at the cars and taxis racing past.

'Hello?' she says again.

I pull out my handkerchief, stuff it over the mouth-piece.

'Police,' I say.

There's no answer. I try again.

'I want the police.'

'Can't hear you very well.'

I take the handkerchief off the phone and hold it over my mouth.

'Can you hear me now?'

I've messed my voice up best I can but it still sounds like a fifteen-year-old boy trying to pretend he's some-one else.

'You're muffled,' she says.

'I need the police.'

To my relief, she puts me through. A man comes on, talking brisk, but I cut him off.

'Write this down. I've only got a second.'

'Can't hear you very well.'

'Forty-seven Abbot Street, you got that?'

'Can you take away whatever you're holding over your mouth?'

I leave the handkerchief there.

'Abbot Street,' I say. 'I was standing by the alley that runs past the back gardens at the bottom and I saw this guy legging it out the back door of number forty-seven. Don't know who he is but he looked really suspicious, like he's just nicked something. You getting this down?'

'It's very hard to understand you. Can you give me your name and telephone number?'

'He's got dark hair,' I go on, 'slick, clean-shaven, smooth-looking guy, about thirty, and he's got this flash coat. It's got—'

A hand clicks off the phone. I spin round in horror to see the man I've just described looking in at me. He's opened the door of the phone box and he's blocking my way out. He watches me for a few moments with a kind of cool amusement, then calmly takes the handset from me and slots it back in the holder. I feel my handkerchief flutter to the floor.

'Glad you like my coat,' he says quietly.

I stare back at him, try to act confident.

'I didn't say I like it. I just said it's flash.'

His mouth smiles; his eyes don't. The traffic goes on roaring past. He steps to the side and I see a car parked by the kerb. Big, shiny motor, two men in the front, near-side door open at the back. Flash Coat nods towards it.

'Get in,' he says.

CHAPTER 3

I step out of the phone box, aware of the guy's hand on my shoulder. It's not gripping me, but I can feel the pressure guiding me towards the car. I walk towards it and feel the hand leave. I stop and it comes back, light but firm. I walk on and the hand leaves again. Closer now, to the open door.

The guys in the front aren't watching me. They're just staring ahead, like they're not interested, like this is no big deal. Maybe it isn't, to them. I stop again, feel the hand return. I look round into Flash Coat's face. The mouth is smiling again, but the eyes are colder than ever. The hand stays on my shoulder, and now it squeezes.

'Get in, boy,' he says.

I hear a car horn close by. The hand lets go but stays close. I look round at the street. There's a taxi trying to pull out a little way down, but another car's cut across him and he's stuck. Another blast from the taxi. The other guy gives him the finger. I look up at Flash Coat. He's checking them, not me.

I duck under his arm and tear off down the street. I don't look round, just keep running. No idea what's going on behind me, then I hear the engine. A soft purr, just to my right, and a moment later I see the bonnet of the car edge alongside me, keeping pace. Same as before: neither of the men looking at me. I check the back of the car.

Flash Coat's not there.

I cut left, into the garage forecourt, run across to the farthest pump, stop, look round. The car's pulled to the side of the street, ticking over quietly as the traffic roars past it. I see the taxi overtake and disappear in the throng. The guys in the front are staring ahead, but here's Flash Coat walking up behind them.

Sauntering even, like there's no rush, like he doesn't want to crinkle his coat. No question he's the guy in control. He stops by the car, leans down. Nearside window opens, guy in the passenger seat says something, Flash Coat straightens up, looks over at me, and now he's sauntering again, this way.

I run round the back of the garage, past the car wash, past the pressure gauge, down to the end of the fence, stop by the gap. It's only small and it'll mess up my school uniform, but I don't care about that. What matters is that bastard's coat. He won't want to squeeze through with that thing on.

He might not even see where I've gone, if I'm quick. He hasn't appeared yet. I push through the gap, and now I'm on the other side of the fence and belting into Ashgrove Park. Only now I can see the car again. It's over to the right, tracking round the street. No sign of Flash Coat but the guy in the passenger seat's watching me through the park railings and talking on his phone.

This isn't going to work. Park's too small and there's only a scrawny little patch of grass and the children's playground and then I'm out in the street again. I stop by the water fountain where the path forks. The car pulls over to the side of the road, the guy still peering at me and talking on his phone.

I'm thinking of Flash Coat again. He's not behind me or following the car. I check the paths in front of the fountain. Seems pretty obvious suddenly. Right fork takes me back to the main road and the guys in the car will cover that. Left fork takes me to the Barrow Street exit, and that's where Flash Coat'll be waiting. Nothing else for it.

I turn and run back towards the broken fence. The guys in the car'll see what I'm doing but I've got to chance it. I might just get through the gap and away before Flash Coat changes direction and comes back. And the guys in the car won't get there for a good few minutes. They can't turn in the road where they are. They'll have to head down to the roundabout before they can cut back.

But even as I race towards the fence, I hear a blare of car horns and—shit! The guys in the car aren't bothering with the roundabout. They've seen what I'm doing and they've just pulled straight out into the road, blocking cars, taxis, buses, everybody. More horns, a great shriek of noise from both sides of the carriageway, but the car's still pulling across, and turning, turning, and now they're round and tearing back towards the garage.

I run on towards the fence, feeling the car in the corner of my eye. They've slowed down again so they can keep me in view, but they'll lose sight of me for about a minute once I'm through the gap, and that's when I've got to decide—out through the garage or back into the park.

I dive through the gap, stop, take a breath, dive back, and now I'm racing into the park again. No idea if this is the right thing to do. Glance to the right: no sign of the car. If they've guessed I've doubled back, it'll still take them a few moments to turn again and come after me. What's bothering me now is Flash Coat. He could be anywhere. I push him out of my head and run on.

Water fountain.

Right fork. Obvious choice. Quickest way out of the park and if I can just get to the main road before anyone stops me, I should be able to run over to the other side and lose them down one of the side streets. Past the children's playground, couple of mothers in there with toddlers in the sandpit, and on towards the gate at the end.

The traffic goes on roaring past to my right, and I'm watching it as I run, checking for the shiny car. No sign of it yet, but they'll have worked out by now that I'm not by the garage and if they got there quick enough to be sure I didn't escape that way, they'll be haring back here again. I glance over my shoulder: still no car.

But now I've seen Flash Coat.

Standing in the gate ahead.

I stop, panting for breath. He's just watching, with that same expression of cool amusement he had back at the phone box. Doesn't bother walking into the park, just pulls out his mobile, taps a number, says a few words, puts his phone away—and there's that smile again. The one that comes from his mouth. I don't look at his eyes. I've already turned and I'm running again, back towards the fountain.

I don't bother checking the main road or back at him. Makes no difference now. They've got me covered whichever way I go. I take the other fork at the water fountain and tear off towards the Barrow Street exit. I won't get out that way. I already know it. Some part of me has given up. The part that's still thinking knows Flash Coat will stay where he is, one of the guys from the car will watch the gap in the fence, and the other one'll be waiting for me at Barrow Street. So there's no point in running.

I do anyway. I might just get past whoever's there. I know I'm fast. It's the one thing I'm confident about. But I'm scared out of my head now. I slow down where the path starts to bend to the left. Can't see round because of the bushes, but I can feel Barrow Street waiting there, beyond the rickety iron gate. I stop, take some more breaths. I can hear the traffic again. I kind of stopped noticing it. There's cars and taxis and motorbikes, a sort of mixed rumble of engines, and then one in particular.

An engine ticking over: a smooth sound I recognize. The only reason I can hear it is because it's close. Maybe there's still a chance. Maybe I can cut back, try another way out. But here's Flash Coat walking up behind me, or sauntering, rather, with that smile. I can see the eyes too now. I wish I couldn't. I turn back towards the exit and walk down the path. The bushes fall away and there's the gate just a little way down, and beyond it the car, murmuring its silky tune.

Driver's still sitting at the wheel, staring ahead like he was before, but this time his mate's got out, and he's standing there watching me as I near the gate. Same kind of face as Flash Coat, only without the smile. I pull open the gate and stand there. The guy leans down, opens the rear door of the car, fixes me with his eyes. I glance left and right, then back at him, and something tells me fast feet won't work this time. Behind me I sense the shadow of Flash Coat moving close.

I step forward, out of the park. The guy nods me towards the open door. Again I check left and right. There's cars and taxis and buses, but this might as well be an empty road. Nobody knows me here and nobody cares. Then I hear a horn further up the street. I turn towards it and suddenly I'm waving.

'Mr Latham! Mr Latham!'

CHAPTER 4

The headmaster's car's still some way off and he wasn't honking his horn at me but at a jaywalker who's stepped out to jink through the traffic. I don't think he's even heard or seen me, but it's enough for Flash Coat. He climbs into the car without a glance or a word, the other guy does the same, and a moment later they're gone.

Mr Latham's car draws closer and now I'm thinking I might be able to avoid him if I duck straight back into the park. But the horn sounds again and this time I know it's for me. I stay where I am and watch as the car pulls over where Flash Coat and his mates just were. The near-side window slides down and Mr Latham leans across.

'Do you have a valid reason for being out of school?'

'No, sir.' I hesitate. 'Do you?'

He gives me a hard look.

'Get in the car, Zinny.'

I climb in but leave the door open. Mr Latham turns off the engine.

'Close the door,' he says.

I close it. The headmaster swivels round in his seat and looks me over.

'Your uniform's a mess.'

'It's been worse, sir.'

'That doesn't redeem it, Zinny.'

I'm not quite sure what he means, but I say nothing. The headmaster frowns.

'So what kind of story are you going to cook up for me this time?'

'For messing up the uniform?'

'For being out of school.'

I shrug.

'Haven't got a story, sir.'

'You just thought you'd take the day off.'

'I suppose.'

'Like you did yesterday.'

'I turned up yesterday.'

'For registration,' says Mr Latham, 'and then you dis-appeared. We didn't even see you for registration today, did we?'

'Can't remember, sir.'

'I can.'

No, he can't. He won't have checked. He's too busy.

'I checked,' he says.

'On me?'

'On you.'

'Why?'

'Because as I explained to your mother and father at our last meeting—'

'I can remember what you said, sir. I was there.'

'As I explained to your mother and father,' says Mr Latham, 'I'm extremely worried about you, Zinny. You're wasting your potential and I don't know why.

17

Up until recently you worked hard, but then you just stopped. You don't even go running any more, except to get out of school. You certainly don't run competitively like you used to. And now you've started truanting, and you won't tell us why. Even though we all want to help you.'

I turn and stare out through the windscreen. The traffic's rumbling past and I find I'm checking cars; checking for that car anyway. I catch a movement from Mr Latham and see him looking at his watch.

'Bit late to take you back to school now,' he says. 'I'll drop you home.'

'I can walk, sir. Thanks.'

I reach for the door.

'Zinny,' says Mr Latham.

I look back at him.

'I'll drop you home,' he says.

He starts the engine without another word. I'm thinking hard. I'm guessing Mr Latham will come with me right up to the front door, but it's just possible Mum'll have too much to think about already to waste time chewing my ear off. That'll kick in later. Unless I tell her what I know about her little fling. I think of Romeo again and those shoes.

Mr Latham pulls out and we move off in the slow lane towards the lights. I'm glad of that. The longer this takes, the better, but now the traffic's picking up speed, and soon we're round the roundabout and heading for the railway bridge. I'm half-hoping the police'll have come and gone by the time we show up.

'Police car outside your door,' says Mr Latham.

Shit.

The headmaster pulls over a little way down from the house. I don't know if it's deliberate, but I'm grateful to him. They can't see us through the window. He switches off the engine and turns to look at me again.

'Anything you want to tell me, Zinny?'

'What about, sir?'

'Whatever you like.'

I shake my head.

'Didn't think so,' he says.

'Sir?'

'Yes, Zinny?'

'Are you coming with me to the front door?'

'I presume that's not a request.'

'Yes.'

'It is a request?'

'It's not a request.'

'You'd rather I just leave you here and drive off?'

'Yes, sir.'

Mr Latham glances at the house, the police car, then back at me.

'What's going on, Zinny?'

'I don't know, sir.'

'Have you been at home today?'

'No, sir.'

'Not at all? You didn't go back to the house once?'

'No, sir.'

'So where did you go today?'

'I just . . . wandered about Ashgrove Park. Where you saw me.'

He doesn't believe this. I can see from his face. But

why should he trust anything I say? I stopped telling the truth some time ago. He's watching me hard now.

'So you've got no idea why that police car's there, Zinny?'

'No, sir.'

'What about those men?'

'What men?'

'By the park entrance. I saw you with some men. They got in the car and drove off just as I arrived.'

'They're nothing to do with me.'

He goes on watching me, then suddenly nods towards the house.

'Off you go, Zinny. I don't imagine my appearance will help things. Your mother and father have clearly got other things to think about right now. But listen . . .'

He leans closer.

'I'll be in touch with your parents about this soon, so I suggest you tell them what you've been up to today, and about my bringing you home. Because I'll certainly be telling them myself. Is that clear?'

'Yes, sir.'

'Off you go.'

I jump out, close the door and stand there by the car. Mr Latham starts the engine but doesn't drive off. I dawdle my way towards the house, but it's no good. I can see he's not going to move till he's seen me through the front door. I walk a bit faster, but not much. He stays there, engine running. I stop outside the front door, reach into my pocket, pull my hand out again, walk back down the street. Mr Latham turns off the engine and climbs out of the car.

'What's wrong, Zinny?'

'Lost my key. I'll go round the back.'

He gives a snort and strides past me towards to the front door.

'Sir! Wait!'

He stops and looks round at me, a knowing expression on his face. It's still friendly, but it's telling me not to push my luck. I walk back to the front door and stop beside him.

'Ring the bell, Zinny.'

'Sir—'

'Or I'll do it for you.'

And he reaches for the bell. I thrust my hand quickly over it.

'Ring the bell,' says Mr Latham, 'or use your key.'

'I just told you I lost it.'

'Why don't you have another look for it?' he says. 'Who knows what's hiding in those pockets of yours?'

I pull out the key and glare at him. His face doesn't change and for a moment it reminds me of Flash Coat, with that quietly amused expression he had. Only if Mr Latham's amused, it doesn't last long. He steps straight back to his car and stands by the driver's door.

'Go inside, Zinny,' he says.

There's no point fighting this any more. He's going to wait there till he sees me go in. I push the key in the lock, turn it, walk in. From outside comes the roar of the car as Mr Latham drives off. I close the door and turn to see Mum standing in the hall.

CHAPTER 5

'What the hell are you doing here?' she says. 'It's too early for you to be home.'

'Too early for you too.' I can't help saying it. 'You're supposed to be cleaning offices.'

'We've had a break-in.'

Maybe she thinks that's the only answer I need. And maybe it is. Maybe lies are all we need for each other from now on. A policeman and a policewoman come out of the front room and stand behind Mum. She hears them but doesn't look round.

'This is my son Zinny,' she says.

'Nice to meet you, Zinny,' says the man.

I give him a nod. Mum keeps her eyes on me.

'We've had a break-in,' she says.

'You just told me.'

'Don't think they've taken anything, but they made a bit of a mess. I think I might have disturbed them. I came back this afternoon—'

'Why?'

'Why what?'

'Why did you come back? You were meant to be at work.'

'I had a headache,' she says.

I wonder if the two police officers know she's lying as easily as I do. Even if I hadn't heard her with Romeo, I wouldn't believe her now. She's always worked hard, specially now the rent's gone up and we're more skint than ever. She'd never come home for a headache. She pops a cigarette in her mouth, fumbles in her pocket for the lighter. I pull the cigarette out and crumple it in my hand. She looks up at me sharply.

'You don't want a cigarette if you've got a headache,' I say.

She puts another cigarette in her mouth, lights it, blows out the smoke. I see the police officers shift on their feet. It's easy to guess what they're thinking, but I don't care. Mum doesn't look bothered either. She's watching me close.

'You been at school today?'

'No.'

Might as well tell her. Before Mr Latham does.

'Why not?' she says.

'I had a headache.'

No reaction.

'Mr Latham just dropped me off,' I say.

'How come? If you weren't at school.'

'He saw me outside Ashgrove Park. He was in his car.'

'Seems like everyone's out of school today,' says the policeman.

I don't answer this. Neither does Mum. Not sure she even heard him. Or maybe she's just not interested. Hard to read her face right now. The policeman steps forward.

'We'll be on our way, Mrs Okoro,' he says.

The policewoman walks up and joins him, then looks at me.

'Zinny,' she says, 'how long since you were last in the house?'

I give a shrug, but it doesn't do much good. The question just comes back.

'How long since you were last in the house?'

'Since I went out this morning.'

'What time was that?'

I see Mum watching me close again. She takes another drag of the cigarette, flicks the ash in the cactus pot, goes on watching. I look back at the policewoman.

'About eight,' I say. 'When I went off to school.'

'Except you didn't go.'

'Right.'

'So where did you go?'

'Not here.'

'Zinny!' says Mum. 'Answer the lady's question.'

It's hard to know where to look now. They're all staring at me.

'I didn't come here,' I say, 'if that's what you're all thinking.'

The policeman glances at his notebook.

'Somebody phoned the police earlier this afternoon,' he says, 'somebody trying to muffle his voice, apparently. But it sounded like a teenage boy, they said.'

Mum's still watching me. No change of expression. I'm guessing they've already told her about the phone call. The policeman looks up at me from his notebook.

'The boy claimed to have seen a man running away from this house.'

'Yeah?'

'Was it you who made the phone call?'

'No.'

'Where were you this afternoon?'

'Wandering round Ashgrove Park.'

'The whole afternoon?'

'Yeah. And the morning.'

'Bit boring, surely?' says the policewoman.

I look at her.

'Why?'

'Tiny little park with nothing to do.'

'I like the children's playground. I like going on the roundabout and swings and playing in the sandpit.'

'Are you trying to be funny?'

The woman's eyes have hardened. So have Mum's. She turns to the two police officers.

'No point asking Zinny any more,' she says. 'That's all you're going to get out of him.'

I've got a feeling they don't believe her, but the policeman nods.

'We'll keep in touch, Mrs Okoro,' he says.

And with a glance at me, he steps out the front door. The policewoman follows and closes it after her. Mum stares at it for a moment, then turns and slaps me in the face. I give a yelp, take a step back. Mum stubs her cigarette out in the cactus pot.

'You little liar!' she snaps.

'You're lying too.'

'Oh, am I?'

25

I glare at her. I've got Romeo in my head again. He stood here with her, right by the door. I can almost smell him. Maybe it's his scent lingering on her. I watch her snarling at me and I want to scream out what I know and dare her to deny it. But I see another slap coming. I catch her wrist this time.

'Let me go, Zinny!'

'Only if you promise not to hit me.'

'I'm not promising anything.'

I let go anyway, but watch her hand. It stays by her side, quivering. I take another step back and we stand there, glowering at each other. Then she reaches in her pocket and pulls out another cigarette.

'You're not supposed to be smoking, Mum.'

'What's it got to do with you?'

She lights the cigarette, blows out the smoke, leans against the door.

'So I'm lying, am I?' she says. 'How am I lying?'

She's changed suddenly. She's acting confident, acting angry, but she's feeling neither. I know her too well. She's wondering if I know about Romeo and I'm not sure I'm ready to tell her. Or maybe I just don't want to. Not yet anyway. I frown.

'I just know you haven't got a headache.'

I watch her hands again, but there's no slap. She just blows out some more smoke, then pushes past me and disappears in the front room. I wait a few moments, then walk in after her. She's slumped on the sofa, staring towards the wall. There's a mess of junk on the floor from the drawers the guy pulled open.

'Going to take a while to put that stuff back,' she says, not looking at it.

She's draped herself across the middle of the sofa. I walk up to her.

'You going to hog that whole thing?'

She makes space for me. I flop beside her and she reaches an arm over my shoulder.

'Little shit,' she says.

'Shut up, Mum.'

She pulls me closer. I dip my head into the crook of her neck, trying to forget Romeo's dribbly mouth being here earlier. She kisses my hair. I put my arm round her waist and give her a squeeze. She takes another drag of the cigarette, then gives a cough.

'Got to give these bloody things up,' she says. 'They're doing me no good.'

'You didn't use to smoke that many.'

'I didn't use to do a lot of things.'

I hear the sound of a car outside and tense up. It moves on and I relax again.

'You're jumpy,' says Mum.

'Don't like the house getting broken into.'

She says nothing.

'So what did the police reckon?' I say.

'They didn't reckon anything,' she says. 'They're not interested.'

'They said that?'

'Course they didn't say that. They said all the usual stuff, like they're supposed to. But they're not interested.'

'Why not?'

'Because nothing was taken,' says Mum, 'far as I can

tell. The house has been roughed up, but I think I disturbed whoever it was and they legged it. Policeman made a few notes but I couldn't tell him anything was missing, so what are they going to do? When there's break-ins all over the city, and real stuff getting nicked.'

'He said they'd keep in touch.'

'They won't.'

Another car engine outside. I try not to tense up this time. I feel Mum glance down at me, then turn away to stub out her cigarette. The engine ticks over for a few moments. It's not Flash Coat's car, I can tell that, nor Dad's van, but now it's moving off again. I take a slow breath and try to go on acting calm.

'You're still jumpy,' says Mum.

I glance round at her. She looks old suddenly. I never thought about it till now. I used to love it when I was a tiny kid and I saw her waiting outside the little primary school at the end of the day. She'd stand by the gate with all the other mums and even though I was only six or seven, I knew she was better-looking than the others. A proper woman. She's not like that now. Or maybe she is. Romeo must think so. So maybe it's me. Maybe I've changed.

'Mum?' I say.

'Yeah?'

'Have you told Dad about the break-in?'

'Tried to.'

'What does that mean?'

'Rang him but I couldn't get through.'

'Where's he delivering?'

'God knows,' she says. 'They send him everywhere, don't they?'

'So you texted him?'

'Yeah.'

Mum pushes me away and stands up.

'Better start sorting this lot out,' she says. 'They made a mess of the main bedroom too. Go and have a look if you want. But come back and help me here, can you?'

'I'll go up later.'

We tidy up in silence, put everything back as it was, sort of, then head upstairs. Mum and Dad's bedroom's worse than the front room. I remember the sounds I heard—and I was right. The guy had pulled up the carpet and started working away at one of the floorboards when he was disturbed.

'Christ knows what they thought we've got under there,' says Mum. She knocks the board back in place. 'Come on. Let's finish off in here.'

We push down the carpet, nudge the bed back into position, tidy as best we can, and by supper time things are more or less like they were. Except they're not. Because deep down I know everything's changed, and not just for me. Mum's not the same. She cooks me an omelette, chats about stuff, even jokes with me a bit, but she's far away in her head. By ten o'clock in the evening it's like she's forgotten I'm there.

By eleven o'clock I'm wondering why Dad isn't home.

CHAPTER 6

Night-time, and someone's watching my window again. Can't make out who it is, just that it's a man. He's standing further down Abbot Street, other side of the road, just in the shadow of the wall. But it's this house he's interested in. No question. I've been watching him close as I can. He hasn't moved once out of that shadow, but I've felt his gaze. I've got questions pounding my head now.

First about Dad. Half past midnight and still not back.

Second about Mum. Why doesn't she care?

She just shooed me off to bed and brushed away questions about Dad. He'll be back, he's just busy, he's been sent on a long delivery job, he's driving back through the night, or he's pulled over to have a sleep. No, it doesn't matter that he hasn't texted back or rung, you know what he's like with mobiles.

Yeah, I do, Mum. He's good with mobiles.

But nothing, nothing, nothing from Mum and so I'm sent off to my room and told to get into bed. Only I'm not in bed. I'm in my clothes and on my feet and I've been staring out of the window since I got up here. Because that guy's been out there all the time, and I wonder how much longer. Maybe he's been here all evening, while Mum and I were eating and talking. We had the curtains closed and I didn't check outside. Didn't want to. And Mum didn't check either. You'd think she'd have been looking out for Dad. She used to once.

The guy still isn't moving.

This is stupid. I can't keep Mum out of this any more. I walk out of my room and over to hers. Door's closed. I stop, lean close. No sound of breathing inside. I ease open the door, put my head round. She's lying on her side on top of the bed, in her day clothes. Hasn't even kicked off her shoes. She's not asleep either. She's just lying there. She fixes her eyes on me.

'What's wrong, Zinny?'

'There's a guy in the street.'

'Doing what?'

'Watching our house.'

She sits upright, looks at me for a moment, then climbs off the bed and walks over.

'Show me.'

I take her through to my room.

'Just peep round the side of the curtain,' I say. 'He'll see you otherwise.'

'Stuff that.'

She pulls the curtain right back and stares down the street.

'Other way, Mum.'

'There's somebody down by the railway bridge.'

She's right. There's a man down the other way too, right back in the shadows near the bridge. Can't believe I never spotted him. But I guess I was fixed on the first guy.

'Look the other way, Mum,' I say. 'There's a guy there too. That's the one I was talking about.'

She looks the other way, and there he is, still there.

'Can't see his face,' says Mum.

'But he's watching the house, right?'

She doesn't answer.

'Mum?'

'What?'

'What's going on? We get broken into and then Dad doesn't come back, and now there's two guys hanging round outside the house.'

'How long's this one been there?'

'Long enough.'

Mum sets off towards the door.

'What you going to do?' I say.

She carries on without a word. I hurry after her and catch her arm.

'What you going to do, Mum?'

'What do you think I'm going to do?' She gives me an impatient look. 'I'm going to have a word with him, find out if he's got a good reason for standing there gawping at our house, and if he hasn't, he can piss off.'

'Mum, don't be stupid. Ring the police.'

'What for?' she says. 'I told you they're not interested. And they won't come out here again just to check some guy in the street.'

'Two guys.'

'Makes no difference.'

'Mum, stay inside.'

'I don't like that git watching our house.'

She heads downstairs to the front door and starts shrugging on her coat. I grab hold of it and try to pull it off her.

'What are you doing, Zinny?'

'Don't go out there, Mum.'

'Get off me!'

She tugs her coat free and buttons it up.

'Stay here.' She looks me over. 'Get the phone and take it up to the window again. Make sure you're standing there with the light on, so he can see you watching with the phone in your hand. If it looks like I'm in trouble, ring the police.'

'I won't. I'll come running out.'

'You'll bloody ring the police.'

She gives me a kiss.

'And then come running out.'

'Mum—'

'Don't stop me, sweetheart. I'm going to do this.'

And she opens the door and steps outside. I grab the phone and jump back up to my bedroom. Mum's already half-way down the street, striding towards the guy in the shadows. He hasn't moved, hasn't turned and walked off, like I hoped he would. I stand there, watching, like Mum told me to, then I remember what she said about the light. I run over and switch it on, then hurry back to the window. The guy doesn't look this way. Don't think so anyway. Hard to see from here. Pretty sure he's watching Mum, and she's close to him now.

Move, you bastard, walk away, go somewhere else. But he doesn't. He just stands there, watching her draw near. Then, to my relief, she stops, out of reach, but only to start talking. Can't hear a word from here but I don't need to. She jabbing her finger at him, getting worked up like she always does, much too quick, and I don't like this, because he's not doing anything, he's just standing there like a statue, watching her, letting her speak. Then his hand slips into his pocket and comes out again.

And I'm racing down the stairs. I hear the shot before I reach the front door. I burst out into the street. Mum's on the ground, sprawled on her side, the guy standing over her, his gun pointed at her head. His face is still dark with shadow but his body looks calm and relaxed, like this is all normal, like it doesn't matter if anyone hears or sees him. But no one else is out here at the shit end of Abbot Street.

There's lights on in the houses further down, but no one coming to help. I hear footsteps somewhere behind me and glance round. It's the guy Mum saw hanging round the railway bridge. He's running away and soon disappears. I turn back to Mum. She hasn't moved since I last looked and neither has the gunman. But he does now. Towards me. I crouch, duck my head. I'm too scared to look at him. But I manage to shout.

'Go back!'.

Like he cares.

'Go back!'

I hear him come on, closer, closer, then catch the sound of an engine. I feel the gunman brush past me and run off. I look up and see headlights looming in the night. I make myself check the other way but the gunman's already disappearing under the railway bridge. I turn back again and a van pulls up by Mum's body.

It's Dad.

CHAPTER 7

I hate the hospital. I hate the gloomy night-time deadness of the place. It's not dead really, not here at A and E.
There's police outside and in here there's nurses ghost-
ing about, and people sitting waiting on the shabby seats,
an old woman in a wheelchair being pushed away, two
guys in beds stuck down the corridor like sad little ships
waiting for a tide, and then there's me and Dad, sitting
by a door they won't let us through.

Don't know if Mum's dead. She wasn't when they
rushed her in, but she wasn't conscious either, not from
the moment me and Dad got to her, or in the ambulance,
or through the hospital to this stinking little door. What
she's like now I don't dare to think. I just know she was
taken through there half an hour ago and nobody's come
out since. All we've had is a nurse come by to check
we're all right, and then she buggered off.

Too much to do, I guess. For all the deadness of this
place, there's trouble coming in on top of ours. I can hear
voices down the corridor even now, drunken voices—
been a fight probably, bottle in someone's face. Who
cares? They can't help Mum. I look at Dad. We haven't

spoken since he drove up. He just rang for the ambulance and then everything happened too fast, and now it's happening too slow. Sitting here, worrying about Mum.

I should say something, though.

'Where were you?'

He turns his head and stares at me. He looks wasted. I try to tell myself it's all because of Mum but something nags in my head that it's more than that.

'Working,' he says.

'That all I'm getting?'

'How much more do you want?' He glances towards the door, then back at me. 'Eh?'

'I just want to know what you were doing this evening and where you were.'

'I told you,' says Dad, 'working, earning what I can to pay the bloody rent and put food on the table, all right?' He glares at me. 'Doing what I do six days a week, seven if I can manage it. Delivering parcels round the effing city.'

'But where? You still haven't answered my question.'

'Doesn't matter where.' He glances at the door again. 'Company sends me all over the place. Christ's sake, Zinny, you know this. I don't need you nagging me when we've had a break-in and your mum's got shot. You know the police are going to want to ask you questions?'

'And you.'

'What are they going to want to ask me?' he says. 'I wasn't here for any of this. You're the one who saw what happened.'

'They'll still want to speak to you.'

I look round. Two police cars turned up just after the ambulance and one of them has followed us to the hospital. I check through the window. Guy and a woman standing by their car, the same two officers who came to our house after the break-in. They haven't spoken to us yet, which I guess means they're trying to be tactful and wait till we know about Mum. But they won't wait for ever and I'm going to have to think what to say.

They're walking across now towards A and E. I watch them through the glass doors. Taking their time, quiet and methodical. I suppose this is just another job to them. Someone's got shot, father and son sitting in A and E, ask a few questions, go through the drill, move on. All in a day's work. Why should they care if Mum's dying or dead already? They reach the entrance to A and E, the glass doors open automatically, and they come straight over.

I catch Dad's eye as he turns to look at them, and there's something in it that's not right: not the sulkiness I usually see there, or the danger when he pulls off his belt, but something else. Don't know what. The police officers stop in front of us and the guy gives us a general nod. Dad nods back. I just look.

'I'm so sorry about Mrs Okoro,' says the policeman, 'and I do apologize for bothering you both at a time like this, when you'd probably rather—'

'Go ahead,' says Dad.

'I beg your pardon, Mr Okoro?'

'You've got questions for Zinny. Go ahead.'

'Thank you, sir.'

The policeman glances at the woman.

'We have some questions for you too, Mr Okoro,' she says.

Dad grunts.

'Like what? I wasn't there for the break-in. I wasn't there for the shooting. I didn't see anything. I was driving round the city.'

'You arrived just as the gunman was running off.'

'So?'

'So you might be able to describe him.'

'Zinny had a closer look than I did. Ask him.'

'We will,' says the policeman, 'but I'm sure you'll appreciate, Mr Okoro, that we have to ask you about this too. You might just have seen something that could help us.'

Dad shrugs.

'I got back late. I expected to be home much earlier but I work for a delivery company and they sent me all over the place today. And then I got caught in traffic coming home.'

'Did you know about the break-in, sir?' says the policeman. 'I assume Mrs Okoro tried to contact you about it during the afternoon?'

'She left voicemail messages and sent texts,' says Dad, 'but I didn't pick any of them up till late this evening.'

'I'm surprised you didn't check your phone earlier, Mr Okoro.'

Dad shrugs again.

'Too busy driving, driving, driving. And you people would be the first to pull me over for using a mobile on the road.'

I look away in disgust—and that's when I see him on the other side of the glass doors, just out of reach of the sensor so they don't open: Flash Coat, looking in at me with that cool little smile. He's so confident the others aren't looking his way that he's actually lounging there, like he's got all the time in the world—and maybe he has. Nobody's checking him out. Dad's frowning up at the officers and they're frowning down at him. I turn back to the glass doors and see Flash Coat's still there. Only the smile's suddenly gone. He glances at the police, then back at me, then puts a finger to his mouth, and makes a throat-cutting gesture. I stare back at him. Yeah, mate, I get it. And he knows I do.

Because he's already sauntered off.

CHAPTER 8

They've sent us home. No point staying at the hospital, they said. They've taken out the bullet and she's still alive, but she's unconscious and there's nothing we can do for now. We can go back tomorrow to see how she is and they'll call us if anything happens. They said. So I'm none the wiser about anything, and nor are the police. I told them nothing about Flash Coat and his men. I'm not stupid. I know what I'll get if I talk.

I told them what I remember of the gunman, but it wasn't much. It was dark, he'd been watching the house, Mum went out to speak to him, he pulled a gun on her and fired, I ran out, he ran off, and I was too busy freaking out to see him clearly, all of which is kind of true. Dad didn't say much either, to the police or to me, and now we're back in the kitchen, slumped on chairs, staring at each other across the table, and dawn's nowhere in sight. The kettle switches itself off.

'You make it,' says Dad.

I heave myself up and make the tea.

'There's no milk,' I say.

He doesn't answer. I close the fridge door.

'I said there's no milk.'

'I heard you the first time.'

I put the teapot on the table, fetch the cups, sit down again. All's quiet in Abbot Street, but I can hear the hum of the city further off. I picture those country meadows again, the ones in that book I've got, then Mum lying in the hospital bed, eyes closed.

'Dad?'

'Pour the tea.'

'It's not brewed yet.'

'Pour the tea.'

I pour him a cup. He watches me do it, then glances up.

'You not having any?'

'Too weak.'

I wonder for a moment if I'm talking about him. Something in his face tells me he's read that in my mind. Then he grunts and picks up the cup.

'Suit yourself.'

I watch him drink, his eyes staring down.

'So what do you want to know?' he says suddenly.

He peers across the table at me, cup poised.

'Go on,' he says. 'Ask.'

I hesitate. His hand flies out and smacks me across the cheek.

'Jesus, Dad!'

'Ask!'

'You didn't have to do that.'

'Get on with it.' He lurches to his feet, tips the rest of his tea down the sink, fetches a can of beer from the fridge. 'You got questions,' he says. 'They're written all over your face. You think I'm hiding something from you.'

He rips open the can, slumps back in the chair.

'I'm fed up with it, Zinny, your shitty little mug gawping at me like I'm some criminal.'

I rub the side of my face. Dad takes a swig of beer.

'So get on with it,' he mutters. 'Ask your bloody questions.'

'I just wanted to know where you went today.'

'I told you back at the hospital. I've been all over the place. What's wrong with you? Do you want to see my delivery sheet or something?'

'If you've got it.'

'Well, I haven't.' He glares at me. 'So tough. You'll just have to believe me.'

'Why haven't you got it?'

I see his right arm twitch.

'Don't hit me again, Dad. I'm just asking.'

He settles his arm, takes another swig of beer, wipes his mouth with his sleeve, then struggles to his feet again.

'I'm going to bed,' he says. 'I'm wiped out and Christ knows what's going to happen with your mum tomorrow.'

'Today.'

'What?'

'Today. It's four in the morning.'

He stares down at me for a few moments, glowering, then staggers off. I hear the sound of his footsteps on the stairs, then more steps into the main bedroom, then a thump as he falls on the bed. A few minutes later, the sound of heavy breathing. I glance at the teapot, my empty cup beside it, then stand up, walk out of the kitchen and stop at the foot of the stairs.

I can picture him sprawled on the bed in his clothes. Didn't hear him put down the can so he's probably splashed beer over himself too. Wouldn't be the first time he's done that. Once he even vomited over himself and still went to sleep. I'm not going up to check he's all right. I can't bear the sight of him right now. Still don't know why I love the bastard. Maybe it's because of his good days, but they don't come around so often now. Same as with Mum.

I push open the front door, stare outside. No sign of anybody. Abbot Street's quiet, this part anyway, like it normally is. The neighbours might as well not exist, even at a time like this, or maybe especially. No one's rung the bell, no one's checked we're OK. Even the landlord didn't show up. Typical. Mum gets shot and no one gives a shit. They just close the curtains, lock the doors, let the Okoros sort out their own crap. Nothing to do with us, mate.

'Yeah,' I murmur to them, 'nothing to do with you.'

I pick up the keys to Dad's van, close the door behind me, step outside, listen. Drone of traffic from the top end of Abbot Street; an early train rattling over the railway bridge, heading for the city centre. I walk over to Dad's van, stop by the door, check over my shoulder. No light on in Dad's window. I unlock the van door, climb onto the driver's seat, peer at the dashboard. Too dark to see clearly. I flick on the interior light and stare at the milometer. Hundred and sixty-seven miles since yesterday.

More than he did the day before but he's still averaging about a hundred and fifty a day since I started checking two weeks ago. I look back at the house again. I always feel guilty doing this, but I can't help it. Hundred and fifty miles a day. It kind of fits with what little he tells me, but it also kind of doesn't. Not quite sure what I mean by that. Maybe just that miles aren't only a number. It's where they take you that counts. Maybe he always did a hundred and fifty a day. Maybe it's cool. But I don't think it is. I don't think he ever did that many. So Christ knows where he's going during the daytime.

I switch off the interior light and a shadow falls over me from the side of the van. There's a guy standing by the door, a guy I don't know. Another shadow, second guy, other side. The door whips open. First guy grabs me by the scruff of the neck. I open my mouth to scream but a hand plugs it. The second guy's here too now and they're bundling me off round the back of the van, down the little track from Abbot Street towards the waste ground. I'm half-running, half-stumbling, moaning like shit.

'Too much noise, kid,' says one.

I go on moaning. They stop suddenly, face me.

'Too much noise, kid.'

I don't see the fist. It just piles into my stomach. I bend over, gasping, and now I'm flung over the guy's back, coughing and bouncing as he carries me on, past the waste ground, over to the fence and down along it to where the railway bridge stretches over us, dark and silent; and there's Flash Coat, waiting.

With a smile.

CHAPTER 9

Even down here the man looks perfect. He's standing in front of a big clump of nettles with the rusty fence on his left and dog shit on his right, but it's like none of that can touch him, like none of it would dare. The guy who's been carrying me throws me down, luckily on a clean patch of ground. But that's the only luck I'm getting here.

Flash Coat leans down. He's wearing black, shiny gloves. He grabs me by the hair, squeezes it, yanks me up to my feet, and now he's drilling me with his eyes. I try not to flinch, but it's no good. I'm trembling and he can't miss it.

'All going wrong, boy, isn't it?' he says.

Same smooth voice, same silky confidence. He's still smiling, hasn't stopped smiling once, but his eyes are like cold stars.

'Bunking off school,' he murmurs, 'and now your mum's been shot.'

The smile fades and there's mock-sympathy there instead, then that fades as well and something else comes, something I haven't got a name for; a new voice too, quieter, more dangerous.

'But first we need to find out how much you've been talking.'

'I haven't been talking, mister.'

'Let's find out.'

He nods to the two guys. I look round in a panic, but they've already grabbed me by the arms. They shove me back against the fence, one either side of me. I feel the dewy metal pressed against my spine. Flash Coat looms closer and suddenly I'm gabbling.

'I haven't been talking, mister.'

'Don't believe you.'

'I haven't said a word.'

'Don't believe you.'

He nods again to the other two. They pull my arms to the side, holding tight. I'm talking faster than ever now, the words tripping over each other.

'I'm telling the truth, mister. I promise I am. I haven't said a word.'

'Course you've been talking.' Flash Coat pulls out a knife. 'I would if it were me. I'd tell everyone what I've seen. My mum, my dad, the police.'

'I haven't told them anything.'

'Strip him,' he says to the men. 'I hate liars.'

'Please, mister—'

'Strip him.'

They rip off my pullover, my shirt.

'That'll do for the moment,' says Flash Coat.

They push me back against the fence again. It's cold and wet and hard. Flash Coat edges close, his eyes on mine. I glance down, searching for the knife. He's holding it behind his back. I don't want it there. I want it where

I can see it, not coming at me blind. The other two yank my arms out again. I look back at Flash Coat and beg.

'Please, mister. I haven't said a word to anybody.'

'Why not?'

'I was too scared.'

'You didn't look scared by the phone box. You didn't look scared when you ran away through Ashgrove Park.'

'I'm scared now.'

He brings the knife round in front of my face.

'Even if you didn't talk,' he says, 'I can't take the risk of you living.'

I try to move back from the blade but the fence won't let me. I'm trembling so bad now I can hardly speak, but I mumble something.

'I didn't say anything, mister, not to Mum or Dad or the police or anybody. I saw you outside the hospital when you gave me that signal. I got the message. Talk and get killed. I got it. I promise I got it.'

'You told the police about me. I heard you on the phone.'

'But they didn't understand me. I promise they didn't. I had a handkerchief over my mouth. You saw it. I was trying to disguise my voice. Only they couldn't get what I was saying, none of it. The guy said so. The guy at the other end.'

Flash Coat shakes his head.

'I still can't take the risk.'

'I won't talk, mister.'

'I know you won't.'

'Please don't kill me.'

He watches me calmly. Jesus, this guy's cold. I reckon he could cut me into pieces for fun and forget about it

47

by the end of the day. His eyes run over me and I start to wonder what he really wants. I've suddenly got a feeling it's more than just my blood.

'So what if I let you live?' he says suddenly. 'What do I get?'

'Me keeping my mouth shut.'

'Oh, that won't be enough.'

He strokes the knife over my cheek. The blade feels chilly and smooth. He twists it slightly, so it chafes my skin without quite cutting it. The smile comes back, goes away. Not sure which is worse.

'And anyway,' he goes on, 'I still don't believe you. I could let you live and you could still go and blab. So let's think about your mum and dad. What if something happened to them?'

I don't speak.

'What if your mum gets better,' he says, 'and they let her out of hospital? And then a few days later she's found on a refuse tip with her throat cut?'

'But—'

'And then your dad goes missing too. And someone finds his van, and there's been a terrible accident.'

'Mister—'

'Because that's what's going to happen, boy.' Flash Coat leans close, the cool blade between us. 'That's what's going to happen if you breathe a word about any of this. Your mum and dad'll both die, and it won't be pretty, because I'll make sure of that. And when we've done with them, we'll come looking for you. Trust me. That's what'll happen if you talk.'

'I won't talk, mister. I won't say a thing.'

He turns the blade so it's pointing straight at me, the tip pricking the skin between my eyes, and then he peers along it into them. I see his gloved hand tighten round the shaft of the knife, feel the blade ease inwards—then it stops and he pulls it away and steps back.

'Like I said,' he goes on, 'that won't be enough.'

He glances at the two guys and they let go of my arms. I drop them to the side, take a long breath. I'm still trembling bad, but I keep my eyes on Flash Coat.

'Here's what's going to happen,' he says.

A train thunders over the bridge above us. Flash Coat waits till it's gone, his eyes on me as calm as they've been all along.

'You're going to search your house,' he says. 'You're going to have a good, long look, and you're going to do it in secret. Because we don't want anyone else knowing, do we? We don't want Mummy and Daddy getting ripped up and killed just because you cocked up.'

'What am I looking for?'

'You'll know it when you see it.'

'Can't you tell me what it is?'

'I don't need to. You'll recognize it straightaway. It's something you wouldn't expect to find in that pisshole of a house you live in. It's something that shouldn't be there. But I want it. And you're going to bring to me.'

'But I don't know what it is.'

The gloved hand whips out, the one with the knife. He's holding the blade flat so it doesn't cut me, but it slaps into my cheekbone and drives my head round against the fence. He pushes harder still and I feel my face thrust into the gap between two of the posts. I'm choking and terrified he'll ram it all the way through. He doesn't but I hear his voice in my ear.

'You'll search your house,' he breathes. 'You'll do it in secret. You'll look in every hiding place. And when you find what I want, you'll tell me.'

'What if I don't find it?'

'You'll tell me that too.'

'How do I get in touch with you?'

'Tell Spink you want to see me.'

'How come you know Spink?'

Flash Coat pulls me back, jerks me round so I'm looking at him again.

'I know everyone,' he says, 'even your school bully.'

'Spink's the reason I don't go in. He beats me up.'

'He won't when you tell him I sent you.'

I look down, try to think of a way out of this, but I know there isn't one. Except to do what this guy says. I feel the gloved hand again, under my chin, pushing my head up—and there's the smile swallowing me. I try to look back but all I see is the chill of the eyes in that beaming face. I manage to speak, somehow.

'What do I call you when I see Spink? I don't know your name.'

He lets go of me, steps back, straightens his coat, though he doesn't need to. Nothing's out of place. He dusts himself off anyway, then looks back at me.

'Think of a name for me,' he says suddenly.

'Flash Coat.'

'That'll do,' he says. 'Call me that. Spink'll know.'

He nods to the other two.

And they're gone.

CHAPTER 10

The house looks the same, but everything's different now. It's like my whole life's been turned over. Don't know what to think about anything or who to trust, if anyone. I put the keys to the van back in Dad's pocket and walk up the stairs. Don't need to bother creeping. He won't hear me. He's snoring so loud I reckon nothing'll wake him.

He's lying on the bed just like I pictured him, face down, clothes on. I was right about the beer too. Can's lying next to him, on its side, stain on the duvet where it's spilt out. I walk in, take the can, put it on top of the chest, then pull open the top drawer. Might as well start now. Dad won't know anything about it. He's just lying there like a plank.

Nothing in the top drawer, nothing Flash Coat might be looking for anyway. He's probably been through this already. I reckon he had time before Mum disturbed him. I check the other drawers: nothing. Dad rolls over on the bed but doesn't wake. I bend down, peer underneath. Just shoes under there, all dusty. Don't know why I'm wasting my time here. Flash Coat checked all this.

I straighten up. Light's filtering through the window. I walk over to it and stare out. The city hum seems louder already. I think of Mum in the hospital, and Flash Coat, and Spink of all people waiting, just for once not to beat the shit out of me, and I think of the thing I'm meant to be taking him, if I can just find what it is; and then I think of this tosser of a father sprawled on the bed with secrets of his own locked in his head.

God knows what he's getting up to during the day-time. I almost don't want to know. He rolls over again but still doesn't wake up. I walk through to my own room, check everywhere I can for the thing I'm supposed to recognize. Nothing, so I check downstairs, dragging myself from room to room, knackered out of my head now, and still shivering at the memory of Flash Coat's threats, and still I can't find anything. I stumble back to my room and throw myself on the bed. Next thing I know, someone's shaking me by the shoulder.

'Zinny.'

'Piss off!'

'It's nine o'clock.'

It can't be. It was dawn just a moment ago. I feel a slap on the cheek and open my eyes to see Dad leaning over me.

'Wake up,' he says. 'It's nine o'clock.'

He slaps me again.

'And don't tell me to piss off.'

I wipe my eyes and peer up at him.

'You look like shit,' he says.

'So do you.'

'You should have got undressed and got into bed.'

'You didn't.'

He doesn't answer this, just straightens up and rubs his face.

'You need a shave,' I say.

'No time for that. We're going to the hospital. Get moving.'

I struggle off the bed.

'Any news of Mum?'

'I rang the hospital,' he says. 'They said we can come in.'

'Is she OK?'

'She's been shot, for Christ's sake. Course she's not OK.'

'But she's alive?'

'She's alive and we can talk to her, they said. But we can't stay long.' He looks me over. 'Splash your face and tidy your hair. You look like you've been in a fight. I'll get something for you to eat on the way.'

Don't know why he bothers. The something's a dodgy apple. But he's got nothing so I guess I'm one ahead of him. We get in the van and I wait for him to start the engine. He doesn't. I peer ahead towards the top of Abbot Street and go on waiting. Still nothing. I glance at him. He's hunched over the wheel, smoking.

'We going or what?' I say.

He starts the engine and we set off.

'Can you lower the window?' I say.

'What for?'

'Smoke's driving me nuts.'

He lowers the window, flicks some of the ash out, glances at me.

'I phoned the school,' he says. 'Told 'em you weren't coming in today. Not that they ever expect you.'

'Did you tell them about Mum?'

'I said she's had an accident.'

'Is that all?'

'Yeah.'

'Have you rung the cleaning company?'

'You can do that,' he says. 'I haven't had time.'

'What's the number?'

'It's on a card in the glove compartment.'

I find it, pull out my mobile, punch in the number.

'Don't tell them she's been shot,' says Dad. 'They might knock her off their list of cleaners. Just tell them she's not well but she'll be back soon.'

'Matrix Cleaning Company,' says a voice in my ear.

I give a start. There's no mistaking Romeo.

'Matrix Cleaning Company,' he says again.

'It's Zinny Okoro,' I say. 'I'm ringing on behalf of my mum. Dana Okoro.'

'Yes?'

No change of tone, no intake of breath. I wonder what he thinks of her, if anything.

'She won't be coming in today,' I say. 'She's had an accident.'

'Oh, I'm sorry to hear that.'

No, he's not, the bastard.

'Nothing serious, I hope,' he says.

'She's been shot.'

I see Dad turn sharply in the driver's seat and glare at me. There's a silence at the other end of the phone.

'She's been shot,' I say again.

Romeo's voice comes back.

'That's terrible. I'm . . . so sorry. Is she . . . ?'

'She's alive,' I mutter. 'Me and my dad are on our way to the hospital.'

'I thought I could hear an engine.'

He doesn't give a shit. I can tell. He just wants to get me off the phone.

'Do give her our best wishes,' he says. 'Tell her we hope she gets better soon.'

I ring off before he can say any more. Dad yells at me straightaway.

'You stupid kid! What did I say to you? I said don't tell them she's been shot!'

I shrug. Makes no difference. They won't be employing her again, and I don't want them to. If Mum comes through this, the less she sees of Romeo the better. Dad turns back to the wheel, glowering. I watch him for a few minutes, not sure about the next bit. But I've got to risk it.

'Dad?'

'Now what?'

'Have you rung the delivery company?'

'Why do you want to know?'

'I could ring them for you if you want. Tell them you're not coming in.'

'I can do that.'

'But you're driving.'

'And you're driving me nuts,' says Dad. 'Just lay off talking, can you?'

* * *

The hospital's as miserable a place as it was last night. They take us through to see Mum. She's awake and she's

55

alive and I guess that's what matters, but she looks wiped out. No talk in her, apart from tiny stupid stuff. Did I get any breakfast? Did someone ring the cleaning company to say she's not coming in? Did someone ring the school? She doesn't ask about Dad's work, and now they're hurrying us out again, almost before we've arrived. Mustn't tire her, they say, must give her the rest she needs. She's out of the danger zone but she's got to stay in hospital under observation. They say.

But Mum's not the only person under observation.

CHAPTER 11

I felt it in the van coming here. Being followed, being watched. I've got nothing to back that up. Couldn't even say I saw a strange car in the wing mirror or a motorbike tailing us, just felt we were being tracked all the way from Abbot Street to the hospital. Even while I was on the phone, I felt it, even while Dad was grumbling and glowering, and now we're back in the hospital car park, I feel it again.

'So what's up with you?' Dad says.

'Nothing.'

'You keep looking round. Settle down, can you?'

But Dad's jumpy too, however much he's pretending he's not. We climb in the van but it's the same as when we got in earlier: he doesn't start the engine, just sits there hunched over the wheel. I glance round the car park. Plenty of cars coming and going. Nobody looks suspicious, so I guess they all do. Dad certainly does, and maybe it's him these hidden people are watching, not me. I stare at him. He's still hunched over the wheel and he's frowning hard, like it's the only way he can keep his secrets from spilling out.

'What's going on, Dad?'

'Nothing.'

'Why did we get broken into?'

He doesn't answer. I think of this mystery thing Flash Coat wants me to find for him, the thing he's ready to kill for; and I think of my lump of a father, sitting here like a turd and avoiding my eyes.

'Why did we get broken into, Dad?'

'Listen,' he says, 'lots of houses in Abbot Street have had burglaries.'

'How do you know?' I say. 'You never speak to the neighbours.'

'Lots of houses in Abbot Street have had burglaries,' he goes on, like saying it twice will sort the thing out, 'and this time they tried us, OK? Turned the place over a bit and ran off, and then later some piece of scum was hanging about in the street and for some reason best known to herself your mum decided to go out and talk to him. God knows what she thought she was doing. Should have left him out there. And it turns out he had a gun and was ready to use it.'

Dad glances round the car park.

'But it doesn't mean there's some great plot against our family,' he goes on. 'It's just means there's scum out there. But we knew that before.'

He starts the engine.

'I'll get you home,' he says.

'I want to go to school, Dad.'

He looks at me like I'm off my head. Which I maybe am.

'You serious?' he says.

'Yeah.'

His face changes. He almost looks concerned.

'I don't reckon you should,' he says suddenly. 'I mean, with all that's happened, don't you think—'

'I want to go to school. And you've got to go to work.'

I try to see his eyes shift—and they do, just a bit. Then they're back on me again.

'You're not in your uniform,' he says.

'Drive me home and I'll change. I can make my own way to school.'

'No, I'll drive you there.'

He really does look concerned now. Something else too. Guilty maybe. He drives out of the hospital car park and down to the traffic lights. They're on red. He stops, lights a cigarette, glances at me. Lights turn green and we drive on. Dad lowers the window again and flicks out the cigarette ash.

'You are going into work, aren't you?' I say.

'Wasn't going to,' he says. 'I was going to stay home with you.'

'But they'll be expecting you. They'll have deliveries ready for you. And you haven't rung in, you said.'

'I'll sort that. It's nothing for you to think about.'

He shoots me a look, and it says shut up about this. But I can't.

'Will you go in to work now I'm going to school?'

He doesn't answer.

'Will you?' I say.

'Christ's sake, Zinny.'

'We need the money, Dad.'

'Don't tell me what I know,' says Dad, 'and don't tell me how to do my own job.'

'I'm not.'

'I'll sort my own stuff out. I don't need you bugging me.'

I stay quiet for the rest of the way back. We turn into Abbot Street and park outside the house. Dad switches off the engine and leans back in the seat.

'I'll wait here while you change.'

I go into the house, close the door behind me, listen. All quiet. I walk from room to room, go upstairs, check round. I was half-expecting to find the place turned over again. But maybe Flash Coat doesn't need to do that now he's got a terrified little kid doing the searching for him. I hear the horn outside and walk to my bedroom window.

Nothing happening. Van's just parked there like it was. Dad's not even looking at the house. He's lighting a new cigarette from the butt of the old one. But he prods the horn again. Well, he can wait till I'm ready. I'm not hurrying just because he's edgy. I check the rest of the street. Nothing suspicious: just everything. I felt watched all the way here from the hospital and I'm pretty sure I'll be watched all the way to school.

Or Dad will be.

The horn sounds again. Bloody hell. I change into my school uniform, cut downstairs again and out into the street. Dad's peering out of the van window. He catches sight of me and stabs a finger at his watch. I climb back in the van.

'You took ages,' he says.

'So what? You're not busy today.'

'I've got things to do.'

'You said you weren't going into work.'

60

'Put your seat belt on and hurry up.'

We drive down to the railway bridge and take the turning towards the city centre. Ashgrove Park opens on my right. I think of Flash Coat again, and his yobby men, and the yobby boy who's waiting for me at King Edward's School. But the first person I see there is Mr Latham. He's standing inside the school gate talking to the caretaker. He sees the van coming in and moves to the side, then spots me in the passenger seat and waves to Dad to stop. Dad pulls over and Mr Latham walks round to his window.

'Mr Okoro,' he says. 'I'm so sorry to hear about your wife's accident. I do hope she's all right.'

'She got shot,' I say quickly, before Dad can invent something else.

Dad glares at me again but Mr Latham gives a start.

'I had no idea,' he says. 'That's terrible. I'm so sorry.'

'She's in hospital,' says Dad. 'We've just been to see her.'

There's a silence, like Dad doesn't know how much to say and Mr Latham doesn't know how much to ask. The caretaker looks blankly on. I catch Mr Latham's eye.

'She's still alive,' I say, 'but she's weak.'

'And do they think—'

'She's going to pull through.' I feel my voice waver for a moment but I make myself talk on. 'She's going to pull through. They've got the bullet out and she's going to pull through.'

'Of course she is,' says Mr Latham. He looks back at Dad. 'There's no need for Zinny to be in school today, Mr Okoro. Absolutely no need at all.'

'He wanted to come in.'

Mr Latham looks at me again.

'I want to come in,' I say.

'I see.'

Mr Latham waits while Dad parks the van, then tries again.

'You're quite sure about this, Mr Okoro?'

'It's what he wants.'

Another look from Mr Latham. I nod.

'Very well, Mr Okoro,' says the headmaster, 'I'll make sure Zinny's looked after and I promise we'll ring you if there's any cause for concern.'

I watch Dad drive off again, then feel Mr Latham's eyes on me again.

'I'm going to give you a note to carry round, Zinny,' he says. 'You're to show it to each of your teachers today. I'll come with you to your first lesson.' He checks his watch. 'Where would you normally be right now?'

Anywhere but here, I'm thinking.

'French in Room 10.'

'Who with?'

'Mrs Jeffrey.'

'I'll come with you.'

We walk into the school and down the corridor to Mr Latham's office. He writes a note, then steps out again and we head for the Foreign Language rooms. The school's quiet and Mr Latham doesn't try to talk. I'm glad of that. But he stops me outside Room 10.

'Now, Zinny,' he says quietly, 'I want you to keep this note on you all day and show it, as I said earlier, to each of your teachers. It's just to explain to them that your mother has had an accident and they're to be aware that you're upset but have come in to school anyway. Read it if you like.'

'Don't need to, sir.'

'All right,' he says, 'but there's another thing, Zinny, and it's very important. I want you to remember that you can come and find me at any time if you feel you can't get through things. I'll be in my office most of the day. If for any reason you need to talk, just go to my secretary's office and tell her you need to see me. Is that clear?'

'Thank you.'

'I'll just have a quick word with Mrs Jeffrey before you go in.'

But French doesn't go well. Mrs Jeffrey's fine, no fuss, no explanations to the class, but they're all looking at me with questions. I start wondering how much they already know. Science is worse, and then it's lunch time and I can't put it off any longer. I've got to find Spink. But Spink finds me first.

As usual.

CHAPTER 12

He grabs me from behind, pulls me back round the side of the changing rooms, and there's the big face, leering. He pins me back against the wall.

'Missed you the last few days,' he murmurs, 'but never mind. We can make up for lost time.'

'I got a message for you.'

'Got one for you too, tadpole.'

He rams his knee up between my legs.

'Ah!'

I half-fall onto him. He shoves me back against the wall.

'I got a message,' I try again.

He pushes my face up so he's staring into my eyes. I stare back, aching round my groin. Least it's just him for the moment. But the others won't be long. They're never far from the big guy. He hisses into my face.

'So what's the message, tadpole? Be quick about it.'

'From Flash Coat.'

'Who?'

'Flash Coat.'

Spink's eyes run over me, horrible little dots. I've

seen them so many times. They never quite fit the mon-
ster who owns them. Two years older than me, bigger,
stronger and a thousand times nastier, but he's got these
tiny little specks for eyes. They still scare me though.
They go on running over me, darkening as they move.
He's not going to buy whatever I've come to tell him. I
brace myself for the next bit of punishment.

'Flash Coat?' he says suddenly.

'He said I could call him that. He said you'd know
who I mean.'

I'd hoped he might hesitate when I said that, or even
pull back, but he doesn't. He just keeps his left hand
wedged into my neck, forcing me back against the wall,
and now he's pulled out his mobile with his right, and
he's texting. Doesn't talk, doesn't even look at me. I keep
quiet. Not worth trying to get away. If this goes wrong,
he'll beat me up worse when he finds me later. He probably will anyway. There's no way he'll get an answer
from Flash Coat that quick. But almost at once Spink's
phone pings with a message. He glances at me for the
first time in ages, reads the text, then looks at me again.

'So what's your message for Flash Coat?'

'I can't find the thing he wants.'

Spink fixes me with his little eyes. I'm wondering if he
knows about this already. Maybe he does, maybe he even
knows about the break-in, but I don't reckon so. He went
for me just now like it's business as usual. His eyes move
back to his mobile, and now he's texting again. Another
pause, while we wait for the answer, the heavy arm still
forcing my head back against the wall. The sounds of
the playground on the other side of the changing rooms

seem as far away as the city centre. Another ping from the phone and Spink reads the reply, then eases his arm away.

'Looks like you're in trouble, tadpole.'

There's no sympathy in the face or voice, but both have changed. Not sure if I like them any better this way. I knew where I was with him before. Now I'm not sure where this is going. He turns his head and spits to the side, then looks me over again.

'You'll just have to earn it all back, kid.'

'Earn what back?'

'Whatever you took.'

'I didn't take anything.'

'Then someone else did. And you're going to have to pay for what they done. Tough shit, eh?'

I hear steps behind me and a moment later, as expected, I'm surrounded. Denny pushes close.

'What's this?' he says. 'Some bogey fallen out the sky?'

He reaches out to grab me, but Spink pushes his hand aside.

'Not now, Den.'

'Eh?'

'The boy's with me.'

'You what?'

'Zinny's cool,' says Spink. 'For the moment.'

Denny looks at me, then Spink.

'You serious?'

'Yeah,' says Spink. 'Problem?'

Denny doesn't answer. Spink glances round at the others.

'Jem? Simple? Natty? Anybody got a problem?'

They all shrug.

'Denny?'

Denny shrugs too.

'Long as we ain't got to be mates with the bastard.'

'Nobody's got to be mates with him.'

I feel Spink's arm slip round my shoulders.

'Except for me,' he says. 'I'll be looking after Zinny for a bit. Just to keep him on the straight and narrow.'

'His mum's had an accident,' says Jem.

'Yeah?' says Spink. 'Too bad.'

Didn't take long to get round the school. Probably someone heard Mr Latham talking to Mrs Jeffrey outside the classroom. He thought he was whispering but his voice always carries.

'She got shot,' says Jem.

'Nasty business,' says Spink, like he didn't know any of this.

I hear another text ping in his mobile. He takes his time reading it. I feel the others watching him and watching me. They don't like this any more than I do, but no one's going to cross Spink. He's still reading. Either it's a long text or he's just making a point. Maybe both. I catch Denny's eye. He wants to beat me up so much. I wonder if he knows Flash Coat too, if the others do, if they're all part of whatever Spink's got going here. I wonder a lot of things. Spink punches an answer, sends it, puts his phone in his pocket, smiles at me.

Same smile as Flash Coat.

A smile without friendship.

'Let's have a walk, kid,' he says.

He guides me away from the changing rooms. The others start to follow but he nods them away.

'Wait here. I want to have a talk with little Zinny.'

I see the anger in their faces and Spink must see it too, but he just laughs and walks me on to the fence that runs along the top of the playing fields. A group of younger kids pick up their football and run back towards the school buildings. Spink watches them with amusement.

'Jumpy, aren't they?' he says. 'Anybody would think I'm dangerous.'

He stops me by the gate into the first of the playing fields.

'You got work to do, tadpole. Or people are going to get hurt. People you care about.'

I don't answer. I just want him to tell me what I've got to do. So Mum and Dad can live.

'So here's the bad news,' he goes on. 'Flash Coat's angry with you. No, correction. He's not angry with you, he's hopping-bloody-mad. Cos you haven't found what he wants. But don't worry. There's good news.'

He leans on the gate and grins at me.

'I've told him what a fast runner you are.'

CHAPTER 13

I get through the rest of the school day somehow. Don't really notice it in a way, or not much. I notice people keeping back from me, not just in the old way, me not having any friends and all that, but in a new way, because the story's gone round about Mum. You'd think that'd make one or two come over and say something nice, but nobody does. There's just this big glass bowl round me that moves as I move and everybody else gawps in at me, stuck in their embarrassment or fear or dislike or whatever it is that keeps them back.

Apart from the teachers. Some of them are OK, to be fair. I guess Mr Latham's note helps, though he's obviously said something too, because hardly any of the teachers seem to need to read it. They're nice to me, though, and that's something, and the other good thing is nobody's trying to force me to talk, and I really need that right now, because Spink's stuff is doing my head in. I go over it again and again. It just terrifies me more each time I think of it. There's so much that can go wrong, and so much that hinges on Dad.

Or rather, on what state he's going to be in tonight.

It should be a no-brainer. There's only usually one state Dad's in when he's home for the evening, but he's got to turn up at the house first, and there's no guarantee he'll do that. If he doesn't, or if—amazingly—he stays sober, I'm in the shit. I need him home, and drunk, and sleeping his head off by midnight, and staying that way all through the night. But Dad's never going to be predictable.

He's not waiting for me at the end of school. I guess that was predictable. He never said he was coming to get me, just dropped me off this morning and buggered off. I suppose with any other father, a decent one anyway, we wouldn't need to have a plan. He'd just come back and I'd know he was going to be there, but my dad's not there, course he's not. I never expected him to be, and if he thought I was going to get a bus home like I sometimes do, it doesn't seem to have occurred to him that I might need some money for the fare.

I feel in my pocket. Don't know why I'm bothering. An old hankie and my door key and that's it. I stand by the school gate, watching the buses rumble out, the cars come and go, the other kids walk or cycle past, chatting to each other, like they've got a life that's worth something. Maybe they're not all like that. In fact, I know they're not. There's kids here like me, kids with no friends and no hope of friends, and probably shit as bad as I've got, but I can't help them and they can't help me.

I turn and walk back in through the school gate, then round the side of the building to the bike sheds. This might not work. The thing might be gone and I'm not nicking anybody else's, but it's there, right at the end, the bike Denny's been using for the last two days, the bike he nicked himself, or so I've heard him boast. If he's still hanging about the school and he sees me take this, I'm in trouble tomorrow, even with Spink's so-called protection. But there's no sign of him. I check round, slip over to the bike, check again.

Just a few other pupils walking past the sheds. I reckon I'm safe. Denny wouldn't stick around after school; he'd be out the gates quick as he can go, and if he's not interested in using his stolen bike, then I am. I check the wheel—no lock, as I expected. He wouldn't care enough to find a lock for it. I pull the bike free and turn it round towards the school gate. Rickety old thing, but it'll do for now.

I hop on, pedal fast and I'm soon out in the main road. No one's called after me and although there are still pupils milling about, there's no sign of anyone showing interest in me, and most of all, no sign of Denny. I ride down to the traffic lights, cut left into Newton Lane, then left again down Western Parade. Too busy here, too much traffic. I cut off quick as I can and keep to the quieter roads, even though it takes longer. Can't afford to be seen by anyone who'll report back to Denny. As I ride, I find myself wishing Denny was the only thing I need to worry about.

Crappy old bike, this. Rusty wheels, rusty frame, pedals falling apart. Don't suppose the original owner's that bothered it got nicked. I reach the top of Abbot Street and stop. Cars parked on either side but nothing further down where we live. I wait a few moments, searching to make sure. Don't know what I'm expecting. Nothing really. If Flash Coat or his mates are anywhere near, they're hardly going to park their motor out in the street where everyone can see it. I start to ride down, keeping slow and tucked in close to the kerb, except where I have to swing out round the parked cars. Something pulls up ahead, just outside our house.

I stop, watch, but it's nothing. A delivery van, but without the delivery. The driver's pulled over to check his mobile and now he's driving again. I pedal on towards our house. The delivery van draws closer, then past me and away. I think of Dad, delivering parcels round the city, or supposed to be, and wonder for the thousandth time where he is. Not at home, that's for sure. He parks out in the street and there's no sign of his van. But there's something else. I stop again and peer at our house. Something just moved past the front room window, the shape of a figure inside.

And now it's gone again.

CHAPTER 14

I don't know who it is. Couldn't make anyone out clearly, just the shadow of someone. I go on watching, in case it comes back, but nothing appears. A guy, I'm certain of that, and not Dad, certain of that too: first because of his van not being here, second because it just wasn't him. I think of Flash Coat again, and his dodgy mates, and look about me. Nobody moving this end of Abbot Street. I check over by the railway bridge, searching for more shadows, but there's nobody there either. I look back at the house. Can't go in, stupid idea, and yet . . .

I can maybe find out who's inside without getting caught. If I catch a glimpse through another window. I push off again and pedal past the house, keeping my face turned the other way. Down to the end, round the corner, up to the alley behind the back gardens, stop. I'm breathing hard now, checking feverishly round. I can see the back of our house from here, down along the row, and the north-facing window from my room, and the one from Mum and Dad's. If the guy's in either of those rooms, he can see me through the window as easily as I can see him. Got to hope he's still downstairs.

I leave the bike by the kerb and set off down the alley. All's quiet, apart from the sound of a train over by the railway bridge, heading out of the city. For a moment I wish I was on it. I creep down the alley and up to our back door, then hear footsteps behind me. I whip round and brace myself, but there's no one near, just a boy out in the street. No idea who he is, never seen him before: kid about my age, shock of black hair. He's nicking the bike. I watch him go, then turn back to the house.

Wasn't him I saw inside. I know that for certain. I walk past the back door, keeping low. I'm hoping I can get a peek through the kitchen window. If the guy's in there, I might be able to see him, and still have time to run if he comes for me. I creep to the grimy edge of the window. It's got bird shit on it but I've got to put my face as close as I can. I stay low, lean forward, peer through into the kitchen, and there's the figure, over by the far wall, and I can see now who it is. Mr Bloody Coily. I let myself into the house and stomp through to face him.

'What are you doing in here?' I snarl.

Can't believe how angry I am. I dislike the landlord at the best of times with his smirky, superior manner, but seeing him checking over our house when we're not there makes me want to jump on him. He looks at me with his dead eyes.

'I can do what I like with my own property,' he says.

'You can't just come in without our permission.'

'I'll do whatever I want,' he says, 'and you people certainly don't have any right to complain.'

'Meaning what?'

'You're behind with the rent—again.'

'The rent?' I say. 'Is that what this is about?'

'It is.'

'So what you looking for? Money? Did you check under the carpet? Or behind the fridge? Could be something there, you never know. Mind you, we've had a burglary so there might not be anything left.'

'Zinny—'

'Or maybe you're looking for something you can take away and sell. The TV's got to be worth a bit.'

'Not enough to pay what you owe me.'

'But you thought about it, right?'

Mr Coily stares at me for a few seconds, then shrugs.

'I was looking for one of your parents,' he says eventually.

'You won't find my mum. She's been shot.'

'Yes, I—'

'In case you didn't know.'

'I did know, I do know,' he says. 'I was sorry to hear about it.'

His face and his voice tell me how deeply, how desperately sorry he is. He goes straight on, like we never even mentioned Mum.

'I was looking for your father.'

'Did you ring the bell?'

'I beg your pardon?'

'Did you ring the bell?'

Mr Coily's face hardens.

'I rang the bell,' he says in a low voice, 'and nobody answered.'

'Which means nobody's here. So there was no point you coming in.'

'That's not what it means at all, young man,' he says. 'I'd never assume there was nobody in just because nobody answered the door. Do you think I was born yesterday? I might trust some of my other tenants but I wouldn't trust anyone at this house.'

'There's nobody here,' I mutter, 'apart from you and me.'

We glare at each other in silence. There's something different about Mr Coily today. Can't work out what it is. He's always been slimy, Oily Coily and all that, though I've never said it to his face. Maybe I should, but not here. Got a feeling I've said too much already, being pumped up and everything, and now I've worked out what the difference is in him. For the first time ever he looks dangerous.

I don't think he's going to attack me, but there's something scary in his bloodless face. Maybe he's in trouble himself, maybe there's others not paying their rent. Got no idea how much money he rakes in. I know he's got quite a few properties, but if they're all as shit as ours, he won't be coining it, and if other people aren't paying him either, he'll be in no mood to mess around. He moves suddenly, towards the door. I don't try to hold him back, but he stops again, half-in, half-out of the room, and glances back at me.

'I don't like threatening a boy,' he says, 'but your dad's not here, so it'll have to be you.' He runs his eyes over the kitchen, then fixes them back on me. 'Tell your dad I want the rent by the end of the week, not just this month's rent but everything he owes me.' He pauses. 'And tell him if he doesn't pay up, I've got people who'll make him.'

And with a slam of the door, Mr Coily's gone. I realize I'm shaking. I stand there, try to calm down, try to think. Can't do either. I pull a chair over and sit on it, take some long breaths. Sound of a car pulling up outside the house. I jump up again, peer out the window, but it's nothing, just a taxi hovering, no one getting out or in, driver lighting a cigarette, and now he's moving again. I watch him go, and find I'm still shaking. I run upstairs to my room and fling myself on the bed, curl up, breathe, breathe, hold in the tears. I'm not going to cry. I'm bloody not.

I don't, and after a while my breathing slows down, and the shaking stops. I stretch out, roll onto my back, stare up at the ceiling. Just what I didn't want on top of everything else, Oily Coily chucking threats at us, and he means them too. I just know it. He's never said anything like this before, and I reckon he's desperate, and Dad's pushed him too far this time. He knows people, he says, and I believe him. Like we weren't under siege before. Only I can't think of Oily Coily. I've got to think of Flash Coat, and what Spink's told me to do tonight. Dad'll have to deal with Oily Coily.

If Dad ever turns up.

CHAPTER 15

He's not here by seven; he's not here by eight. I'm starving and there's nothing to eat in the house, nothing decent anyway. Mum would have gone shopping today if she hadn't got shot, and Dad's never going to think of buying anything. I wander round the house, waiting, fretting about what's coming later, my stomach chafing and grumbling, then I hear the van outside. Sounds like Dad's. I slip over to the window and peer round the side of the curtain. Yeah, it's him, just locking the van and now he's coming over, and yep, what a surprise, there's a lurch in his step.

He didn't even wait till he got home to start. Wonder which pub he went to on the way back. Or maybe there wasn't a way back. Maybe he just went there straight after dropping me off at school and he's been there all day. Wouldn't put it past him. He's carrying something, though, and it looks like a takeaway, only—Jesus!—he can't even manage that right. He's got a takeaway for one, I'm sure of it. He sees me watching at the window and jerks his head in the direction of the front door.

'Open it yourself,' I yell.

Takes him a minute of fumbling to get in.

'Why didn't you help me?' he mumbles. 'You can see I've got my hands full.'

'Got nothing to do with your hands,' I say. 'You couldn't manage the door because you're drunk.'

'I'm not drunk.'

'You've been drinking anyway. And you shouldn't have been driving.'

I glance down at the takeaway, check inside the carton.

'Burger and chips for one,' I say. 'Well, that's good. Least we know you won't be going hungry tonight. Who gives a shit about me?'

'I give a shit about you,' he says.

'So why haven't you brought me any food?'

'Bloody hell, Zinny!' He glares at me. 'I'm hardly through the front door and you're on at me!'

'Because you've let me down again.'

'How?'

Can't believe he's surprised. He's got his gob open and he's staring at me like this is all some mystery, like he's been wrongly accused of some terrible crime. His eyes are dark, though, not quite bloodshot—that'll come later—but dangerous enough. He's acting hurt and even a bit meek, but it won't last if I crank him up too much.

'You weren't there after school,' I mutter.

'You serious?'

'You weren't waiting for me. I stood there and you didn't come and get me.'

'I can't believe I'm hearing this.' He stares at me, his mouth moving like he's fumbling for words. 'I thought I had a grown-up kid,' he goes on. 'I thought I had a son who knows I've got stuff to do during the day—'

'Like what?'

'And who might just have the nous to know that if I'm not there waiting after school to nanny him safely home, it's because I'm busy doing other things and he's got to make his own way back.'

'And how am I going to do that?'

'You jump on a bloody bus, don't you!' He thrusts his face closer. 'Christ's sake, Zinny, how hard can it be to show some initiative? You get the bus back when there's no one to pick you up. That's what you always do. Simple.'

'And when I've got no money for the fare?'

'Eh?'

'When I've got no money for the fare?'

'You didn't have any money for the fare?'

'Course I didn't,' I say. 'I haven't got any money for anything.'

'Then why didn't you bloody say so?' Dad shakes his head. 'I can't help you if you don't tell me things, Zinny. You're looking at me like I've messed up here and it's you who's messed up.'

'Yeah, right. Like with the food.'

'The what?'

'The food, the takeaway.'

He glances down at it. He's clutching the carton, squeezing it. I've got to be careful. I know where this is going, but I might be able to avoid getting hit if I watch his hands. He looks up at me again.

'Listen,' he says.

His voice has dropped. I don't like this. I take a step back. He glowers at me, his eyes growing darker.

'Listen, Zinny,' he mutters, 'I didn't get a takeaway for two because I thought you'd have eaten something already, OK?'

'What am I going to eat? There's nothing in the house.'

'There must be something.'

'Have you looked?'

He doesn't answer, just stares dumbly at the take-away carton. His hands are still squeezing it, tighter and tighter. I picture the burger and chips inside getting slowly squashed. He goes on squeezing. I take another step back. He looks up at me, his face hard and angry, then flings his arm back. I don't have to duck. This one's not for me. With a great roar he throws the carton across the kitchen. It hits the far wall, opens and spills. The mangled burger and some of the chips drop onto the cooker. The rest fall to the floor, together with the empty carton.

'You eat the bloody food!' he bellows.

And he storms towards the door. I keep back and let him go. A moment later I hear him in the front room, rummaging about the cupboard, then there's the clink of a bottle and the heavy sound of him falling on the sofa. I walk to the kitchen door and peer across the hall towards the front room. He's left the door open but all I can see from here is his feet sticking out, and that's fine. Can't bear the sight of his face right now. I call through.

'Mr Coily was here.'

No answer. I try again.

'Mr Coily was here. I found him in the kitchen. He let himself in.'

Still no answer. I take a long breath, walk across the hall to the front room and stop in the open door. Dad's eyes swivel up at me, but he says nothing, just knocks back the bottle.

'Mr Coily was here,' I say.

'I heard you the first time.'

'He said he wants the rent by the end of the week—'

'He always says that—'

'And if you don't pay him everything you owe, he'll send some people round to make you. He doesn't always say that.'

'Go and eat the food.'

I don't move.

'Go and eat the food, Zinny,' says Dad.

I stare at him, unsure what to do.

'Close the door after you,' he says.

I close the door on him and walk through to the kitchen, scrape up the burger and chips from the top of the cooker, and shove them on a plate. I'm not touching the chips on the floor, however hungry I am. I sit down at the table and wolf down the food. It's dry and almost cold now but I don't care. I finish eating, wash things up, clear away the stuff on the floor, and walk back to the hall. Dad's still in there but I can tell from his breathing that he's fallen asleep. I reach for his coat pocket, take out the keys to the van, and slip outside. The milometer blows my mind this time.

Two hundred miles.

'Jesus.'

So he didn't spend the whole day at the pub. What the hell's he's up to? I hurry back into the house and close the door behind me. Dad's still breathing heavily in the front room. I think of Spink's instructions, and then of Dad again. I need him up in his room, not conked out here, but I can't make him move. I check my watch. I've to be patient, somehow. I wander up to my room, throw myself on the bed, and wait.

CHAPTER 16

Five minutes to midnight and I'm in big trouble. Dad's
woken up and moved from the front room to his bedroom, which should be good news, only he's taken the
bottle in with him and he's drinking again. I can hear him
grunting as he swigs it back. This is serious. I need him to
be well gone by now, and he usually is. I listen from my
room. There's nothing I'm hearing that makes me think
he's ready to stop. He could be at this for another hour,
and if he is, then I'm really in the shit.

Then I hear a belch, some shuffly footsteps heading
for the bathroom, and retching. I don't go and see. I've
done that too many times and he'll only expect me to
clear it up. He probably will anyway. He's throwing up
big time now. I go on listening. After a while he stops
and I hear running water, and splashing, and the flush of
the loo, then more shuffly footsteps, heading back to his
bedroom.

'Zinny!' he calls.

I go through. Don't want to but I'd better check he's
all right, even if I do get belted. He looks blasted, but
he's not going to hit me. Couldn't if he wanted to. He's

sitting on the side of the bed, his shirt half-unbuttoned, trousers the same, one shoe on, one shoe off.

'Help me get undressed, can you?'

I undo his shirt. He doesn't do anything, just lets me get on with it.

'Your breath stinks,' I say.

His eyes wobble round at me. There's still anger in them but no fight, not even for me. He gives me a long, dozy stare, then turns his head away and gazes at the far wall.

'Bit of a loser, eh?' he mutters.

'Who are we talking about?'

'Not you.'

I pull off his shirt, start on the trousers.

'I can do that,' he says.

He can't. His hands are like jelly.

'I'll do it, Dad.'

He doesn't argue. His eyes are glazed and he's finally tipping into sleep. I pull the trousers off him, then the pants. He's stopped noticing now. He's just keeled over on the bed. I take off his shoes and socks, and his watch, and the pendant Mum gave him back in the days when she still loved him. He gives a moan and rolls away over the bed, his back to me.

I can't leave him like this. I dig around under the duvet for his pyjamas, find them stuffed almost out of sight, walk round the other side of the bed to reach him better. His eyes are shut, his mouth gaping. I pull his legs apart, force the pyjama trousers over them one at a time. I don't reckon he even feels it. No change in the way he looks or the sound of his breathing. I waggle his legs and push his bum till I get the trousers on him properly, then pick up the pyjama top.

He's curled his left arm up against his face. An inch more and he could suck his thumb. Maybe some sleepy part of him wants to do that. I pull his arm back and slide the pyjama top on that side, then roll him over and fix the other side, and after a bit of a struggle get the whole thing buttoned up. Another struggle and I get the duvet out from under him and draped over as it should be, and then I'm standing back, looking down.

'You drunken git,' I murmur. 'You don't deserve me loving you.'

I think of Mum.

'And neither do you.'

But not sure I mean any of that.

I turn the light off, and the one in my own room, and the one on the landing, and set off down the stairs. I don't need to move quiet—Dad's never going to wake up because of me—but I creep about even so. I stop at the bottom of the stairs and listen again. Heavy breathing above me, and that's it. I switch off the downstairs lights and step out the front door.

Abbot Street's quiet and all's dark at this end of the road. I walk up to the top and turn right towards the city centre. Not that I'm going there. I'll be cutting off long before that. I think of the address Spink gave me. Never been there but I can picture the way. I walk up to the lights and cut into Chancellor Road. Lots of people about, clubbers mostly in little tipsy groups and some more riotous ones, but they don't give me any trouble. Police out too, not getting involved.

No need to at the moment. It's busy but relaxed. I wonder if the city ever goes to sleep. Right at The Memorial Stone, down through the narrow streets that thread up towards the river, but we're not going there. Left again and now the people are thinning out, and the only ones left are the type I don't want to see. Got to watch myself now. Spink told me to keep a lookout. Funny to hear him sounding like he cares when I know he doesn't give a shit what happens to me.

End of Bartholomew Street, and here's the first of the alleys, just like Spink said. Don't know this place at all, and I've never wanted to. Part of me wants to turn and run back; another part thinks of Mum and Dad, and that's the bit that makes me walk on down the alley. Nobody in it, nobody I can see, but it's dark down here and I could be wrong. I get to the end without meeting anyone, but the moment I hit the street on the other side, a figure looms out of the murk.

'Who the hell are you?' says a voice.

Big guy, swaying on his feet. He swings an arm at me. I duck under it and run past. From behind me comes a slurred bellow. I glance over my shoulder but he's disappeared down the alley. I stop in the middle of the street, take a few moments to calm down, then check round me. There's no street sign in sight, but I quickly realize I don't need one.

I've arrived.

CHAPTER 17

I check over the building in front of me. Hunter's Moon. A pub that doesn't look like a pub, Spink called it, but he's got that wrong. It does look like a pub, just the wrong kind of pub. It's trying to look like it's in the country when it's stuck in a dirty city street like this with high walls on one side and a railway line on the other and dingy lampposts all along.

Name's wrong too for a city pub, not that I know anything about the countryside, apart from that nature book I like looking at. There's people in the street. Didn't notice them before. Couple of figures further down, slumped against the wall beyond the pub door. I've got to walk past them if I'm going to follow Spink's instructions.

I start off, keeping to the edge of the pavement. I'm not crossing the street just to avoid them, but I keep an eye on them as I draw near and get ready to run. There's no need, though. They don't even look up. Two women, early twenties, I'm guessing, just plonked there on the pavement, leaning against each other. One murmurs something as I walk by.

I carry on past the door of the pub and stop at the far side of the building. Here's the little side-path Spink told me about. I glance back at the women. They haven't turned to look at me. I check out the windows of Hunter's Moon. All dark, no sign of life. Rest of the street's quiet too.

I look round. Nothing moving in the street. Sound of traffic and the usual city hum but nothing happening here, nothing I can see anyway. I start to wonder if I've arrived too late. Spink said I'm OK till two in the morning. After that they'll come for me at home, and I don't want that, he said. But I didn't need him to remind me. I check my watch.

Half one. I look round again. Houses dark, pub dark, just those two women down the street, and now they're wandering off towards the alley where that drunk went. I take a slow breath and start down the path. Darker still down here, just the side of Hunter's Moon to my left and a rough brick wall to my right, too high to see over. I stop.

There's a smell of poo, like some dog's been down here. I peer about me. No lights on anywhere. I think again of what Spink told me. Follow the path, he said, all the way round. I wait a few seconds for the darkness to clear a bit. The path looks like it bends to the left further down. I walk on, watching for dog shit, and cut round the back of the pub to where the path ends.

There's dustbins and old crates piled on top of each other and a small door into the high wall on my right. To the left is a gate into the pub garden, if you can call it a garden. More like a dumping ground. There's grass in the middle and what I'm guessing used to be flowerbeds, but nothing that looks like it grows any more. Even the grass looks dead. A few tables and chairs scattered about, but not like customers would ever use them. I think again of Spink's instructions, push open the gate, and step inside.

There's nobody in sight. I check round to make sure, then turn back to the pub. The path leads straight to a glass-panelled door in the back of the building. I stare at it, searching for some sign of a light inside. Everything's dark, but Spink said I had to knock. I walk slowly towards it, listening again to the hum of the city, and the cold silence closing around me. I reach the door and stop. Four knocks, Spink said. One, two, three, pause, and four. I raise my hand to knock.

'Make sure you do it right,' says a voice.

I whirl round, searching the garden. There's a guy over by the far wall, sitting on an old beer barrel. Can't work out why I didn't see him first go. About Flash Coat's age, but not so smooth. Dangerous, though. That's all I need to know. I can tell just by looking at him. Something flares in the darkness and he lights a cigarette. Stays where he is, thank Christ, watching me as he smokes, then he nods towards the door.

'Make sure you do it right,' he says again.

I knock on the door: one, two, three, pause, glance back at the guy, four.

'Good boy,' he says.

He's sauntering over. He's slimmer than Flash Coat but he's got that same smug confidence. He stops next to me and looks down, then glances at the door. As if by magic, it opens from within, and there's another

90

guy peering out. Another hard bastard. Looks me over, glances at the slim guy, opens the door wider.

Nobody speaks.

I walk in, feel a hand close over my shoulder, and now it's guiding me down a dark corridor past unlit rooms into the kitchen at the back of the pub, and now down some steps into the cellar. No window here, but there's a light on, and three more men, sitting on stools, smoking. Bottles open on a low table, cards face up like a hand's just been played. The men look up, and one of them's Flash Coat.

'Cutting it fine, boy,' he says. 'Spink told you no later than two o'clock.'

I check my watch. Five to two. I look back at Flash Coat. He smiles that smile, watches me in silence for a few moments, like he's waiting for me to smile back, then his eyes flicker towards the slim guy.

'Give it to him.'

The slim guy holds something out. I stare at it—a small, brown package.

'Harmless enough,' says Flash Coat. 'Take it.'

I take it. Doesn't weigh much. There's no writing on the front.

'Turn it over,' says Flash Coat.

I do as he says. The back's blank too but the package is sealed with staples and heavy tape.

'What do you reckon's inside?' says Flash Coat.

'Don't know.'

'Try and guess. Squeeze it.'

I squeeze the package. There's something inside that feels hard, but it might just be a stiffener to protect something else.

'Don't know,' I say.

'Want to open it and find out?'

I look back at Flash Coat.

'Want to pull off the staples and tape and find out?' he says.

He's still got that smile. He stands up, walks over to me.

'I'd want to know,' he says, 'if it was me. I'd want to take a peek inside and then staple it all up again and put some more tape over it and make it look like I never went in there.' A pause. 'Is that what you want to do, kid?'

'No, mister.'

'Say that again.'

'No, mister.'

'Good choice.'

And he whips out his knife and rips it into the top of the package, rips again, and again, savagely, like he hates the thing so much he just wants to tear it to pieces—and suddenly they're flying everywhere, like little flakes of brown flesh. There's nothing inside the package apart from some stiff cardboard and he's ripping that too, grunting as he works, his face dark with concentration, his eyes on the flashing blade—and then he stops and looks up at me again.

'Good choice,' he says thickly.

He takes a long, heavy breath.

'Because if you do one thing wrong, kid, just one thing . . .'

He picks up some of the shredded pieces and holds them in front of me.

'Then that's your mum's face you're looking at.'
He lets them fall to the floor with the rest.
'And then it's your dad's.'
He keeps his eyes on mine.
'And then it's yours.'

CHAPTER 18

I feel something pushed into my hand. I don't look down. I know it's another brown package. The slim guy's put it there. Flash Coat's still watching me, and I'm watching him. I don't dare look away. His eyes are more dangerous than his blade. He watches me a few moments longer, then turns away, back to the low table, sits down, gathers the cards, shuffles them, deals. Two of the other guys join him, none speaking, none looking my way.

I feel the slim guy's hand on my shoulder, easing me away. I'm glad to go with him. He walks me up from the cellar, through the darkness of the pub and out to the back door, just him and me now. I want him to take his hand away but he doesn't. I look down at the package for the first time. Like I thought—same as the other one, same feel inside, something stiff, like it's protecting something else.

And this time there is a something else.

But I don't want to know what it is.

Slim guy opens the back door, steers me out into the night, stops me. Hum of the city comes back. I've missed it in that stinking cellar. The hand's still clutching my shoulder. I look into the guy's face. He's pulled out a mobile and he's texting something. Doesn't bother looking at me, but his hand stays stuck to my shoulder, like a smell that won't go away. I edge back a bit. The hand squeezes, fixes me so I'm still, even as he goes on texting. Then he looks up.

'They're expecting you,' he says.

He talks on, low voice. The address is easy enough. I don't need a street map. But that's where the easy part ends.

'If anyone tries to stop you,' he says, 'you run. Fast as you can. And we know you're fast. Spink said you was.'

'Where do I run? Back here?'

The slim guy looks amused.

'You don't come back here, kid. Not ever. And you don't talk about it neither. You never been here. You never even heard of Hunter's Moon.'

'So where do I run?'

'You run away. That's what you do.' The slim guy pauses. 'And then you run back again, and you keep running back again, till you get to where you're meant to be going.'

'What if I can't get there?'

'Want me to spell it out?'

I think of Flash Coat's knife and say nothing.

'Off you go, then,' says the slim guy, 'and don't hang about if you care for your mum and dad. And yourself.'

'I just deliver this package where you said.'

'To begin with.'

'What does that mean?'

'You'll find out.' He looks me over. 'Shove the package inside your belt and under your shirt. So it don't show.'

I do as he says. Feels uncomfortable but I can't help that. He checks me over once more, then nods me towards the path. I set off down it but stop at the gate and look back. He's already disappeared inside the pub. I step through the gate and cut round back to the street. All's still quiet and there's nobody about. I check my watch. Just after two. Can't believe I was only a few minutes in Hunter's Moon. Felt like ages.

I feel the package under my shirt. Could be lots of things in there, and I can guess a few straight off, but it makes no difference what's inside. It's trouble, whatever it is. I set off, thinking over the route. The first part's straightforward enough, long as that drunk's not still hanging round the alley. He's not. There's nobody in there. I run down it to the other side, the slim guy's words buzzing in my head.

Don't hang about if you care for your mum and dad.
And yourself.

But if I run too fast, that'll attract attention. I make it a brisk walk, checking round as I go. More of the slim guy's words come back to me.

If anyone tries to stop you . . .

Christ knows who he means. Low-life probably, or maybe the police. Don't know which is worse. The police'll notice a young kid out on his own in the early morning and if I get pulled over and checked, they'll find the package, and that mustn't happen. So suddenly everybody's dangerous.

I keep to the shadows best I can but I'm into Guild Street now and there's lights and lots of people, and a police car parked by the far pavement. I cut off just past the funfair, run round the block and back again to Guild Street, nobody bothering me so far, and as I walk, I think of Mum in her hospital bed, and stupid drunken Dad back home.

Don't suppose he's woken up. He never usually does when he's tanked, and even if he does come round, he probably won't look in my room to see how I am. Can't ever remember him doing that. Well, maybe I can. Maybe there were times. Yeah, there definitely were. When we used to talk football and running, and the future, like there was something to look forward to. And Mum used to come in too sometimes. But I haven't seen either of them for a long time, not like that.

I hear a car horn nearby and move to the inside edge of the pavement. Police car noses past, doesn't stop, pulls over further down where there's two women in high boots and not much else slanging away at each other. Nightclub door's open and there's two heavies standing there watching the women, music pumping into the street. I cross the road and skirt round them, then cut back again.

Still lots of people about, but now I'm heading down Charwell Road, and on to the end, and right along the outside of the park, and it's gone quiet, or it feels quiet, and still, and watchful. Just a few people about but I suddenly want to run again. I keep moving, same fast walk, watching shadows. Nobody comes near, not yet. End of the park fence, stop at the T-junction.

Never been here before but I know where this goes. Left at the junction and down towards the river. Small groups of figures hanging about the corners of the road.

I watch them and they watch me. I walk on, faster than before, on the edge of a run. Two guys slumped against the wall over to the left. They get up as I draw near, sidle out into the road. I run over to the other side, sprint past, check back. They're just standing there laughing, too lazy to run. But now I can see they don't need to. Because there's two more guys further down the street.

Blocking my way.

CHAPTER 19

Mid-twenties, long hair, slimy-looking guys. I stop in the middle of the road, praying for a car, but there's nothing moving. I stare at the two figures. They're checking me over like I'm hardly worth the effort of catching. I feel the package chafe against my stomach. One of them calls out.

'Took your time, boy.'

I'm thinking fast. The slim guy at Hunter's Moon told me nothing about who I'm supposed to meet. He just gave me the address, and that's round the corner in the next street. These two could be nothing to do with the package. The guy who called out gives me a wink.

'We come out to meet you, baby,' he says, 'cos we was worried about you.'

'Dangerous place round here,' says the other. 'Wouldn't want you coming to no harm.'

They both laugh, but they're quickly serious again.

'Give us what you got, boy,' says the first.

I hear footsteps behind me and check round. The other two guys have wandered up too now, and they're not laughing either any more. I make a dash for the other side of the road to try and get round them, but they spread out and block both ways, then move in.

'I got nothing!' I call out.

They push me back against the wall.

'I got nothing,' I say. 'I promise I got nothing.'

One of them leans in.

'But you do got something, don't you?' he says. 'You got something specially for me.'

And he pulls up my shirt and snatches the package.

'There's a good boy,' he says.

The other three chuckle in the darkness, then wander off. The guy who's left glances at them, then at the package, then at me. I check him out. He's got dirty, greasy hair and he smells. He slips an arm round my shoulder like we're best mates.

'You done right, kid,' he says. 'You was told to run if there was trouble. Only problem is you didn't run good enough. You didn't get away like you was meant to.'

'What if I had got away?'

He turns to the side, spits, then looks back at me.

'You'd have come back. Cos you was told to keep trying till you got through. So I'd have still got my present. Unless you got caught by somebody else, which would be bad for me, but far worse for you and your mum and dad.'

He tucks the package under his arm and gives it a pat.

'Cos you'd all be dead, boy.'

'Can I go now?'

He watches me in silence for a moment, then reaches in under his belt and pulls out another brown package. Same size, same type: sealed with staples and tape, no writing. He grins at me, then holds it out. I don't take it. The grin fades.

'Don't make me force you, boy. You really don't want that.'

I take the package. Same feel as the other one. Something inside to stiffen it but no hint of what's in there. The guy's watching me, like he's wondering if he needs more than threats.

'Where's it got to go?' I say.

He gives me the address. Never been there either, and it's nowhere near Abbot Street, but I can find it.

'Can I go home after that?' I say.

'Long as you remember.'

'Remember what?'

'To find Spink at school in the morning. Before he has to come and find you.'

'I might not be in school,' I say. 'Depends on how my mum is. I might be going to the hospital to see her.'

The guy shakes his head.

'You go see Spink, boy, or there ain't no point you going to the hospital. You understand what I'm saying?'

I set off up the road. Can't face this guy any more. He doesn't stop me or call out. I walk on, not looking back. The other guys have disappeared and the street's deserted. I start running, crying too. Don't know where the tears have come from—I thought I was too scared to start crying—but they come anyway, and now I'm racing past the park and across the estate, pictures of Mum's face choking my head, and Dad's too, Christ knows why.

It's a half-hour run to this new place, and I push myself hard. Don't care any more about drawing attention to myself. I just want to get rid of this package and go home. I've already worked out I won't make it to the address. The address is just a direction to go. It'll be like the last one. Someone'll be waiting before I get there.

And someone is.

A woman this time, hard-bitten face from what I can see of it. She's standing in the shadows by the turning into the final street I'm supposed to go down—a miserable little cul de sac, so I'm not sorry to miss it. Not that this woman looks friendly. She calls my name and I stop.

'Come here,' she says.

I look round me. Darkness everywhere, no street lamps, just garages down the left side of the road and a high wall down the right, couple of houses further along, no lights on, and a few parked cars. The woman calls out again.

'Come here.'

I walk into the shadows and she thrusts a hand out.

'Give it,' she says.

I pull out the package, praying she's not going to give me another one back. But she just takes this one, looks it over, then glances back at me.

'Piss off,' she says.

I run back the way I came, fast as I can. The tears have gone now, but the fears are worse than ever. I picture Mum's face again, and Dad's, and then the faces I've seen tonight: the ones I want to forget. But they go on hounding me all the way home.

CHAPTER 20

Four in the morning and Abbot Street's just like it was when I left it. So's the house. Dark, silent, uninviting, like no one lives there. Maybe no one does, not proper living, anyway. I lean against the front door, breathing hard. Don't want to go in, don't want to stay outside. Don't know what I want, except for the bad stuff to go away. I think of the figure who shot Mum and look round. No sign of anyone. Not that that means anything.

I pull out the key, open the door, listen for Dad. No sound of snoring or breathing, no sound of anything. He usually makes plenty of noise when he's sleeping off a skinful. I step inside, close the door, listen again. Still nothing to hear. This doesn't have to be bad, but something feels wrong. I leave the lights off, creep to the top of the stairs, and stop. Door to my room's just how I left it.

I walk to the door of Mum and Dad's room. That's how I left it too. I push it open and check inside. Dad's not in the bed or on it, or anywhere to be seen. I hurry in, check round in case he's rolled onto the floor. Not there. Smell of beer and vomit from the side near the window. I run out onto the landing, charge into my room. Not here, hasn't been in once. I can tell at a glance. Out again, check the bathroom, but he's not there either. Down the stairs, thump, thump, and then I hear his voice.

'Keep the bloody noise down!'

It's come from the front room, more a growl than a bellow, and slurred, like it so often is. I stop at the bottom of the stairs. I know what's happened now. Don't need to go further and look. I glance at my clothes. Don't need questions about them either. I run back upstairs, duck into my room, change into my pyjamas, run back down and into the front room. Dad's curled up on the sofa, clutching an open bottle. Got his eyes closed and I think he's fallen asleep again. Then he opens them and looks up at me.

'What you got your watch on for?' he mutters.

I glance at it, casual as I can.

'Forgot to take it off when I changed into my pyjamas.'

Which is sort of true. He sniffs.

'You look stupid,' he says.

'You look wrecked.'

'Probably cos I am.' He yawns. 'Come here, boy.'

I think of Flash Coat. He called me 'boy'.

'I don't like being called that.'

'Called what?'

'Boy.'

'Get over it.'

Dad flaps a hand in my direction. I think it's meant to be beckoning me. His other hand stays tight round the bottle. Least he's got strength for something. I don't move.

'Come on, Zinny,' he mumbles, 'for Christ's sake.'

'You'll have to make a bit of space. You're sprawled all over the sofa. And I don't know if I want to sit with you. You stink of alcohol.'

'Zinny—'

'And vomit.'

'There's no vomit on me,' he says proudly.

That's true. Give him that. But he still smells of it. He's moving now, trying to get himself upright. Hurts me to watch him. He struggles to a sitting position and leans back with a sigh, then pats the space beside him with his free hand.

'Sit here, boy.'

'Stop calling me that.'

'Sit here,' he says. 'Only get my cigarettes first, can you? Over there. And the matches.'

'There aren't any.'

'In the drawer.'

I fetch the cigarettes and the matches, sit down next to him on the sofa. He lights up, looks for an ash tray. I get up, fetch one, sit down again.

'Thanks, boy.'

'Dad!'

'I'm only joking.'

'Bloody hell!'

I slump against his body, too knackered to care about the smell of him. He takes a couple of drags.

'So have you been at these?' he says.

'Been at what?'

'My cigarettes.'

'No.'

'I'm not angry if you have,' he says. 'I did the same when I was your age.'

'I haven't touched them. Count the ones in the box if you don't believe me.'

'I wouldn't remember how many there were,' he says.

'I haven't touched them, OK?'

He takes another drag, taps the ash into the tray.

'Then someone else has,' he says.

I look up at him. His eyes are bleary but they hold my gaze, just.

'Someone's moved the box,' he goes on, 'while we were out at the hospital.'

'You had them with you on the way there,' I say. 'You lit up. I saw you.'

'Another box,' he says. 'I left this one here before we went out and I haven't touched it since. Your mum obviously hasn't and if you haven't either, then someone else has. Cos it's not where I left it. There's other stuff been moved too. I only just noticed when I came down here.'

I look at him doubtfully.

'I might be drunk,' he says, 'but I'm right about this.'

He stubs the cigarette out in the ashtray.

'So I'm guessing whoever broke in last time has been back.'

I think of Flash Coat again and the thing he told me to look for, whatever that is. Maybe he found it this time; maybe I'm off the hook. But I've got a feeling I'm not. Dad stares at the bottle for a while, then places it carefully on the floor and slips an arm round my shoulder.

'We'll go see your mum in the morning,' he says.

'It's morning now.'

'You know what I mean.'

'We can't go till you're fit to drive.'

'I'm fine,' he says.

'You're drunk. You said so yourself.'

I feel him flex his muscles. He's too far gone to hurt me, but he wants to. Then he relaxes again.

'I'll be fine in a few hours,' he mutters. 'I'm not going to crash the van.' He glances at me. 'Or hit you. Whatever you were thinking just now.'

I don't answer. He shakes his head.

'Go on, Zinny.'

'Go on what?'

'Tell me I'm a shit dad.'

'You're a shit dad.'

'And a shit husband. Tell me that too.'

'You're a shit husband.'

He gives a long sigh, then leans back.

'She's seeing someone, Zinny, your mum is. You listening? She hasn't said anything and I haven't asked her, but I can tell. Do you know anything about it?'

I look away. I'm not ready for this question. Or the answer.

'Zinny?'

'Don't know.'

I'm still looking away. Can't let him see my face. Even drunk he'll spot the lie.

'What don't you know?' he says. 'That she's having an affair? Or the guy's name? Or where they do it?'

The voice has suddenly gone hard. Lost its slur too. I haul myself up from the sofa.

'I got to get some sleep, Dad.'

CHAPTER 21

Ten in the morning and we're driving, sort of. Dad's taking it slow and he's gripping the wheel tight, his eyes bloodshot. He's still half-canned. If he's noticed I've got my school bag packed and my uniform on, he hasn't said anything. But he's had a shave and a clean-up and he's put some decent clothes on. If it wasn't for the aftershave, he'd be almost worth sitting next to.

'So what don't you know?' he says suddenly.

It comes out of nowhere. I wasn't expecting this till later, when he'd woken up a bit. Haven't got an answer ready. I try to sound offhand.

'What do you mean?'

'Your mum and this guy.'

'I don't know anything about it.'

He glowers at me.

'You do, Zinny.'

'Watch the road, Dad.'

'Don't change the subject.'

'You're waggling the van about.'

'Don't change the bloody subject.'

'There's nothing to talk about,' I say. 'You think Mum's

108

seeing someone. I'm saying I don't know anything about it.'

A car horn blares nearby.

'Watch the road, Dad!'

He swerves back into the right lane, then pulls over to the side of the road and stops.

'Zinny, listen—'

'Put the handbrake on, Dad. Turn off the engine.'

He does neither.

'Zinny, listen,' he says, 'I'm in a state, all right? Over your mum, over . . . other stuff.'

'What other stuff?'

'You not going to school for starters.'

'What else?'

'Never mind what else. That's enough, isn't it?'

He goes on before I can answer.

'I can't bear the thought of everything falling apart.' He looks round at the cars racing past. 'I know I've been a useless father and a useless husband, and I don't want to be that any more.'

'So are you going to tell me where you go during the daytime?'

'Jesus, Zinny, lay off that.'

'Are you?'

'Bloody hell!'

He rounds on me, fists clenched, then—with an effort—pulls back, and drives on. I curse myself. He was opening up for the first time in ages and I pushed him too hard, and now he's gone quiet and he probably won't talk again. But as we drive into the hospital car park, he glances at me.

'Sorry about the fists.'

'It's OK.'

'I didn't hit you.'

'You wanted to.'

'Yeah, but I didn't,' he says. 'That's got to be worth something.'

'Like what?'

He parks the car, turns off the engine and looks at me.

'A smile would be nice,' he says.

I can't manage a smile, but I give him a punch on the arm. He gives me one straight back.

'Shit, Dad! That hurt!'

'Did it?'

'Yeah, it bloody did.'

'I didn't mean it to,' he says.

'I only gave you a soft punch.'

'I thought that's what I gave you.'

'You don't know your own strength, Dad.'

His face clouds over.

'Now what's wrong?' I ask him.

He looks away over the car park.

'Just thinking.'

'About what?'

'How I must hurt you bad when I really belt you.'

'You do hurt me bad.'

He turns back to face me.

'I won't hit you again, Zinny.'

'You've said that before.'

'I know I have.'

'Lots of times,' I say, 'and then you get tanked and it starts all over again.'

'I know,' he says. 'I'm sorry.'

He hesitates, then pats me on the arm.

'Let's go see your mum,' he says.

I reach for my schoolbag.

'You don't need that with you,' he says. 'Leave it in the van.'

'I'm taking it.'

'What for?'

'Never mind.'

'Full of secrets, aren't you?'

'Looks who's talking.'

Mum looks worse than last time, but she's awake and the nurse tells us we can speak to her for a few minutes. Dad gives her an awkward kiss.

'You stink of aftershave,' she says to him. 'I suppose that means you were drinking all last night.'

He doesn't answer. Mum looks wearily in my direction.

'Don't I get a kiss from you?' she says.

'I got aftershave on too.'

'No, you haven't.'

I laugh, Mum laughs, Dad shifts on his feet.

'Come here, Zinny,' she says.

I lean down and kiss her. She doesn't reach out and hold me. I want her to but I don't say anything. She picks it up anyway.

'Haven't got the strength, sweetie. Love to give you a proper hug but I can't manage it.'

We pull chairs close and sit down.

'I've already had visitors,' says Mum.

I feel Dad fidget next to me, but he doesn't speak.

'Who?' I say.

'Police first of all,' she says. 'Those two who came to the house after we got broke in.'

I glance at Dad. He's relaxed a bit, but not much.

'What did they want?' he says.

'What do you think they wanted?' says Mum. 'To ask me about the shooting.'

'I thought they'd already done that.'

'I wasn't too bright in the head last time I spoke to them.'

'Did you see the guy clear?' says Dad.

'Not really,' she says. 'It was too dark and he was keeping back in the shadows. Don't remember much about it now. All happened so fast.'

Mum's eye flickers over at me, then back at Dad.

'You must remember something,' he says.

'I remember Zinny telling me there was a man watching the house.'

'Two men,' I say. 'You spotted another guy watching by the railway bridge.'

'Forgot about him,' says Mum.

'But what about the guy who shot you?' says Dad.

'I just remember going outside and talking to him.'

'What did you say?'

'I told him to stop watching the house or we were going to call the police.'

'What did he say?'

'Nothing,' says Mum. 'He just reached into his pocket and I don't remember much after that. Till I came round in the hospital.'

Her eye flickers over me again and this time stays.

'Should have listened to you, sweetheart,' she says. 'You warned me not to go outside.'

112

I reach under the sheet and take her hand. It feels fragile. The nurse comes in and stands there. Mum looks up at her.

'Yeah, I know.'

'I'm sorry, Mrs Okoro. They can't stay too long. You need more rest.'

'They only just got here.'

'You've talked quite a bit already,' says the nurse, 'with your other visitors.'

'Who else came?' says Dad suddenly. 'Apart from the police.'

I look at him. His eyes have gone sharp. So has his voice.

'Who else came?' he says.

'Mr Latham,' says Mum.

I sit up in my chair.

'You kidding?'

'Early bird,' she says. 'First one in here, on his way to school.'

'What the hell did he want?' says Dad.

Mum gives a tired laugh.

'You don't half ask stupid questions. He wanted to know how I was, nothing more than that. He stayed for about five minutes, said how sorry he was about everything that's happened, and that was pretty much it. And then the police turned up and wanted to ask me about the shooting.'

'Mum?' I say.

'Yes, Zinny?'

'Did Mr Latham say anything about me?'

'Only that you don't need to worry about going in to

school while this is going on. Says he'll quite understand if you don't turn up. Not that you've been turning up anyway lately.'

'I'm going in today.'

'You don't have to, sweetheart. I just told you.'

'I'm going in,' I say, 'and Dad's going off to work, and you're going to get better.'

They look at me, both of them, each with a different kind of expression. I can read Mum's easy. It's all soppy. Don't know about Dad's. Could mean anything. But I can't be worrying about that now. I look back at Mum.

'We'll let you get some rest now, OK? But we'll be back later. I promise we will.'

'I'll look forward to it,' says Mum. She glances at Dad. 'And you can bring me that present you forgot to get this time round.'

Dad stares at her awkwardly, but Mum only laughs.

'The flowers you forgot to buy me,' she says. 'They got some here at the hospital. You can get them on the way in. Or maybe a nice card with "Get Well Soon". That woman in the ward over there's got loads of stuff round her bed.'

I don't check to see. Neither does Dad. He just bites his lip.

'Dana, listen,' he says.

Mum rolls her eyes at me.

'Doesn't get it, does he?'

She looks back at Dad.

'I'm joking, you idiot,' she says. 'You don't have to bring me anything, not now, not next time, not any time. I'm just pleased to see you two. That's enough. I don't need a present.'

'I got you a present,' I say.

Mum stares at me.

'You what?'

'I got you a present.'

I reach into my school bag, feel for the familiar book. For a few moments I don't want to give it away, then my fingers close round it and suddenly it's in Mum's hands, and she's staring at the cover, and then at me.

'What's this?' she says.

I don't answer. She looks back at the book, reads the title aloud.

'*Nature Magic*.'

'It's got pictures inside,' I say. 'Nature photos. They're beautiful. I thought they might cheer you up.'

She turns a few pages, reads out some of the captions.

'Lark Ascending, Badgers at Dusk, Moon over Coniston. It's lovely, Zinny.'

She flicks back to the beginning—and her face darkens.

'What's this?' she says.

I feel Dad crane over to see. Mum looks hard at me.

'This book's from your school library.'

'So?'

'It's two years overdue.'

'They don't know I've got it.'

'How come?'

'I nicked it.'

'When?'

'Two years ago.'

Mum and Dad stare at me. I notice the nurse has gone. Mum frowns.

'You've had this book all that time?'

'Yeah.'

She glances at Dad.

'Have you ever seen it?'

He shakes his head. Mum turns back to me.

'How come me and Dad haven't seen this book?'

'I keep it under my bed and only look at it when I'm on my own.'

They're watching me like they've never seen me before, like I'm some kind of ghost. Then Mum says, 'Come here, darling.'

I lean over her, the edges of the book pushing into my chest, and this time Mum's hand reaches up and strokes me on the back.

'Thanks for the present,' she whispers.

She gives me a kiss.

'Now go to school.'

CHAPTER 22

I don't get to look for Spink straightaway. I'm still standing on the school steps watching Dad drive away and wishing I'd said something to break the silence between us on the way here—and then I hear Mr Latham's voice behind me.

'Wasn't expecting to see you today, Zinny.'

I turn round and look up at him. He's standing at the top of the steps by the school entrance. He gives me a smile.

'But you're very welcome.'

He beckons to me, still smiling. I walk up and join him by the entrance. He's holding his arm out like he wants to put it round my shoulder. I suddenly find I want him to, but he just uses it to point towards the entrance.

'Let's go in,' he says.

I follow him inside. He glances towards Reception but doesn't stop.

'Mrs Whiley?' he says. 'Zinny's joined us. Can you make a note, please?'

She nods and we walk on. I've kind of worked out we're going to his office for a chat, but I'm worried sick now about finding Spink. I can't forget what the guy said last night about not wasting time, and it's break in ten minutes and if Mr Latham keeps me talking all through that and then takes me off to lessons, I won't get a chance to catch Spink till lunch time, and that could be serious. But there's nothing I can do about it right now.

'After you,' says Mr Latham.

He's standing at his office door, holding it open. I walk in, still thinking of Spink.

'Sit down, Zinny,' says the headmaster.

He points to the chair in front of his desk. I sit down, wishing I could go. I like Mr Latham and he's being great right now, but I need to be somewhere else. He doesn't sit down himself.

'Would you like something to drink, Zinny?'

'No, thanks.'

'Have you had any breakfast?'

I stare back at him.

'I'm not being funny,' he says, 'but you and your father have got so much to think about right now it just occurred to me you maybe didn't get a chance to eat much this morning, or maybe didn't want to. Would you like me to get you a drink or have a sandwich sent along? I could easily arrange that.'

I try to work out how long it takes to make a sandwich, send it here, and then for me to eat it, and get out. Too long, that's all I know, too long to give me a chance to find Spink. But I so want that sandwich, or rather two or three sandwiches, and a cup of tea, and God knows what else. But it's no good.

118

'Just a glass of water, please.'

'Of course.' Mr Latham opens the door again, puts his head round and calls to his secretary in the next office. 'Mrs Flavell, a glass of water for Zinny, please.'

He leaves the door open and sits down behind his desk. I'm counting the seconds. Seems ages before the water appears, but Mrs Flavell eventually shows up, hands it over with a soppy smile, and closes the door behind her. I take a sip, look at Mr Latham.

'Mum said you called in at the hospital.'

'Yes,' he says. 'I hope I wasn't an inconvenience?'

'She was really grateful.'

'Good.' He looks at me for a few moments, then frowns. 'Zinny, I want you to tell me something.'

'Is it to do with Mum?'

'I don't know,' he says. 'Probably not, but . . . I don't know.'

He frowns again, then leans forward on the desk.

'Zinny, why have you suddenly become so friendly with Ricky Spink?'

I give a start, try to cover it by drinking more water. Mr Latham's watching me close. I take my time finishing the water, then say, 'I'm not friendly with him.'

'All right,' says Mr Latham, 'let me put it another way.'

He's not pushing me hard, but he's stopped smiling.

'Ricky Spink's a big lad and he's two years older than you,' he goes on, 'and let's just say he's not famous for being kind to people smaller than himself. So when I see the two of you talking in what seems a companionable sort of a way over by the playing fields, I'm just a little surprised, that's all. That was yesterday, of course, and . . .'

He pauses, gives a cough.

'To be honest, it wasn't me who saw you. It was Mr Philips, and he reported it to me, but that's not what matters. What matters, Zinny, and what I'd like your reassurance on, is that you're all right and Ricky Spink isn't putting any pressure on you.'

Another pause. I can see him waiting for me to speak, to tell him what me and Spink were talking about. I try to think what to say, but he goes on first.

'Of course if you were just chatting, then it's none of my business what you were talking about, but if you're in trouble, Zinny, and it's something to do with Ricky Spink, or indeed anyone else at this school, then it certainly is my business and I hope you'll tell me about it.'

Yet another pause. I've got to say something this time. If only to get away and find Spink.

'It wasn't anything,' I mumble. 'We were just talking.'

Mr Latham doesn't believe me. He's nodding, like everything's OK, but he's not fooled. He knows what Spink is—everyone in the school does—and he knows what I am. I guess everyone knows that too. I'm the tadpole who's got no friends. So nothing's sorted, even though Mr Latham's still nodding.

'All right, Zinny,' he says quietly. 'I won't push you any further, but if there's anything you need to tell me, about Ricky Spink or anyone else at this school, anything you think I should know—'

'I'm not a snitch.'

'That's not what I'm talking about and I think you know that.' Mr Latham leans back in the chair, his eyes not leaving me. 'I also think you know full well the kinds of things I need to be informed about.'

This time he doesn't give me space to answer.

'I need to know about anyone in this school who's causing you a problem,' he says, 'and you need to have the courage to come and tell me. That's not being a snitch. That's being brave. And it's not just about you, Zinny. Because if someone's giving you grief, then for all I know, that person is giving other people grief too. And I'm not having that in this school.'

His voice has hardened and so has his face. I didn't know he could be scary but for some reason I'm glad he can. It soon goes, though. He checks his watch, then stands up with a smile.

'Break coming up,' he says. 'There's no point in you going to lessons. You might as well wait outside for the bell. What have you got Session Three?'

'English.'

Except I won't be going. I'll find Spink during break, get him to tell me what I've got to do next to keep Mum and Dad alive, then clear off out of here. The bell goes and a few seconds later I catch the usual din of doors opening, shouts, footsteps. Mr Latham looks at me. I look back, then stand up.

'Thanks, sir.'

Seems the right thing to say. He gives me another smile; and that's his answer.

CHAPTER 23

Spink doesn't find me this time and it takes me a while to find him. Five minutes of break left and I'm just starting to panic when I see him, outside, by the bins at the back of the kitchen. He's got Denny, Simple and Natty with him. The others don't spot me, but Spink does. No change of expression, no expression at all really. He just mumbles something to the others and stalks away by himself round the corner of the building.

I hurry out of the door and over towards the bins. Denny turns and sees me, says something to Simple and Natty. They're all watching me now and I wait for trouble. I don't get any, not yet anyway, just the stares and the mockery in the eyes, a few words as I draw close, words I can't catch and don't want to, and then I'm past them and round the side of the building—and Spink's waiting.

'Took your time, tadpole. That hasn't gone down well.'

'I couldn't get here any quicker.'

'Your problem,' he says, 'and you don't want to make it mine too or you'll have my shit down your neck as well. You're making life hard enough for me already. I've been getting texts all morning from . . .'

He stops for a moment and fixes me with his dark little eyes.

'What did you call him last time?'

'Flash Coat.'

'Flash Coat, yeah,' he says. 'Maybe he likes being called that, but I'll tell you one thing, bogeyboy, he doesn't like you not turning up on time. I've been getting text after text from him asking if you've showed up yet, and every time I say no, he gets angry.' Spink grabs me by the collar. 'Angry with me, you bastard!'

He thrusts me away again, his eyes flashing. Never seen Spink like this before. He's always the one in control, the one making other people scared. Never seen him scared himself, and he is, no question, terrified even. He's still looking round him, like he's expecting trouble any moment. I look round too.

Nobody here, back end of the kitchen, but there hardly ever is. That's why I often come here myself. Everyone's on the other side of the building. I can hear the shouts, the thump of a ball being kicked, laughter, a squeal of anger from some girl. The bell sounds for the end of break. Spink looks sharply back at me, and there's that fear again in his face, that terror. I hear his mobile ping with a text. He pulls it out of his pocket, reads the message, punches one back, looks at me again.

'Midnight,' he says, and he tells me the address. 'Don't write it down, tadpole.'

'I wasn't going to.'

'And don't forget it.'

I wasn't going to do that either. I can see it's as important to him as it is to me. He's turned away already, and there's Denny and the others hovering just in view. He joins them and a moment later they've gone, and I'm standing here alone. I don't move. Got to give everyone time to get inside before I clear off. Two minutes and it's all quiet again, apart from the clatter of kitchen noises in the building behind me. I cut round to the little lane where the delivery vans come in, check round me again, then run down it to the main road.

Cars cruising past both ways, but no one's interested in me. I wait for a clear space, check further down to make sure no one's coming out of the main school gate, then run across the road and down Wattling Avenue. I've decided what to do. It's dead risky. Flash Coat said midnight and I'll have to turn up then whatever happens, but there's nothing to stop me checking the place out before then—in other words, right now.

Because I already know that come midnight I won't make it to that address. I'll be met by someone just before I get there, like I was last night by the slimy guy, and again by the woman. So I'm getting a feeling about these addresses and I want to see if I'm right. But I've got to be really, really careful. If I mess this up, I could pay for it bad and, worse still, so could Mum and Dad.

Down to the end of Wattling Avenue and round to the parade of shops by the old cinema. Left takes me in the direction of home. Part of me wants to head straight back there, but I turn right, running over the address in my head. Never been there, same as the other places, but

I know how to get there even without Spink's not very helpful directions. Maybe he half-hopes I'll get it wrong and cop it with Flash Coat tonight.

But I don't think so, not seeing him that scared just now. Don't know what game he's playing here but if he's a big noise at school with tadpoles like me, he's a tadpole himself with Flash Coat and his thugs, and I've got a feeling he needs me on his side. I see a 32 bus pull in ahead. Wish I could get on it but I haven't got any money. An old guy standing at the bus stop stares at me. I can tell what he's looking at: the school uniform's just visible under my jacket. He doesn't say anything, though, and gets onto the bus.

I pull my jacket tighter round me and do up the zip. Don't know why I'm bothering. Everything about me says I'm a school kid. I look down at my bag, think of Lark Ascending and Moon over Coniston. Maybe Mum's looking at the pictures right now. I wish I was. Bus moves off. I watch it go, then walk on. Rain's starting. Grey sky, grey clouds. I think about Dad.

He talked on the way to the hospital and said nothing on the way to school. It was like being with two different people, like he changed into someone else after he saw Mum. Hard to work out what flipped him. All I know is I've never seen him look so uncomfortable. I know he feels a failure, but he could still talk, for Christ's sake. Maybe I should ring him. I pull out my mobile, switch it on. Pings straightaway with a text from Mum. I stop and read it.

Luv u x

'I love you too,' I say aloud.

A woman sitting by the side of the road looks up at me. I take no notice of her and tap a message back.

Luv u 2 do u like the fotos?

Send.

I look round. The woman's still watching me. She smiles suddenly, then gets up and walks off. I think of Dad again and hurry on. Half an hour later I'm outside City Stadium.

CHAPTER 24

Round the back of the stadium, empty turnstiles on my right. Rain's still coming down, not hard but enough to give me a good excuse to put my hood up, which is just what I need. Got to hide my face here in daylight. Whoever's going to be waiting tonight could well be here now and I mustn't be seen twice. I'm getting noticed though. I can see that as I peer out from under the hood.

Plenty of people about, rough faces mostly, and I don't feel safe. Dirty little dives to my left, cafes and bars and other dodgy-looking joints. Road's curving round, following the shape of the stadium. Rain's getting stronger. I'm almost relieved. I pull the hood tighter round me, bend my head down, but now I can't see out so well. Someone taps me on the shoulder. I jump to the side, spin round. Old guy leering at me, blotchy eyes, looks drunk. He holds out a gnarly hand.

'Got nothing,' I say.

He pushes the hand closer. I take a step back.

'Got nothing.'

He lumbers off. I watch him go, make sure he's not coming back, carry on round the outside of the stadium, checking the roads to the left. It's one of these, Spink said, but there's still no sign, just figures lounging in doorways. They're sheltering from the rain but they're sizing me up too. I'm easy meat here, even in daylight and with cars and taxis driving past. Small kid out of school, bag slung over his shoulder. He'll have a mobile and a bit of money worth mugging off him. No one comes forward. But they go on watching.

Silverton Road.

That's the one. Dingy and narrow, broken-down terraced houses either side, bins shoved to the edge of the pavement, one of them pushed over. Motorbike picking its way down. I wait till it's gone past me, then set off. Really got to watch myself now. Mustn't get seen, not my face anyway. The rain's easing but I keep the hood up and my head bent over, just glancing up now and again to check the house numbers.

Ten, twelve, fourteen. It's the other side, the odd numbers. I cross over. Eleven, thirteen, fifteen, only I already know that number eighty-nine won't exist. I can see the end of the street, the T-junction where the next road starts. I walk on, checking the houses: fifty-three, fifty-five, fifty-seven. Sound of an engine somewhere behind me, a smooth, familiar, horrible sound. I keep my back to it, hood still up. I know what car it is and who it belongs to.

I'm shaking at the thought of it but I keep walking. They can't know it's me, they surely can't, not here at this time of the day, but maybe I'm just kidding myself. They've seen me before from behind, they've watched me run away, they probably remember this coat, and the car's still drawing nearer; then suddenly the engine stops.

I walk on towards the T-junction, somehow still count-ing: sixty-three, sixty-five, sixty-seven. Rain's getting bad again.

An alleyway opens up on my left. I slip into it, trying not to look like I'm hurrying, then peer back round the edge of the wall. There's the big shiny motor, well down the street. It's parked on the other side, the side with the even numbers. No sign of Flash Coat but I can see two guys in the front and I recognize them: same two who were in the car when they chased me round Ashgrove Park.

The guy in the passenger seat gets out, pulls his coat up against the rain, then sets off down the street towards City Stadium. The driver starts the engine and the car purrs off, in my direction. I duck into the alleyway, turn my back to the street. The purr grows louder, draws alongside, fades as the car moves past, and then it's gone. I run back to the edge of the wall and peer round again.

The car's vanished but the other guy's still in view, walking down Silverton Road. Then he stops, lights a cigarette, glances round, and slips through the gate of the nearest house, a grotty little place squashed into the terrace. Looks run-down and dirty, but he's going in. Doesn't knock or ring the bell, just opens the door and disappears inside. The rain goes on falling. I go on watch-ing. My mobile pings with another text from Mum.

Luv the pics xxx

I text back a smiley, then ring Dad on his mobile. No answer but I wasn't expecting one. I leave a message on his voicemail.

'Just checking you're OK.'

Don't know what to say to him right now, and I guess he feels the same about me. But I wish we'd tried on the way to school. I didn't like the silence in the van. I think of the milometer again and wonder what it's clocking up today. Another ping in the mobile and it's a text from Dad.

Gonna b late

Nothing more. I stare at the words. He might have rung me so I could hear his voice. If he was free to text, he was free to ring and talk. I stare at the words. 'Late' could mean anything, but I can't be worrying about that now. I peer down Silverton Road. No more coming or going at the house where the guy went. I look left to where I'm meant to be going tonight. Number eighty-nine. The address that won't exist.

I walk on towards the T-junction, counting as I go, and sure enough, the last number is eighty-seven. Where some nice person'll be waiting for me tonight, no doubt. I turn and stare back down the road. Everything tells me it's a bad idea to head for the place where the guy went, but I'm already walking back. Only now the rain's stopped and I haven't got an excuse for the hood.

I keep it up anyway. Going to look suspicious whatever I do. I stick to the opposite side of the road. Here's where the shiny car pulled up. I carry on past, trying not to walk fast or slow, just normal, whatever normal is. Two black guys coming towards me, loose and leggy, digging in bins as they go. I could do without them. I check the little terrace house. It's just a bit further down the road. I don't want to go too close, but I want to see better, catch the number, maybe a clue or something.

Crash!

I look back down the pavement. The guys have tipped over one of the bins. An old man leans out of an upstairs window nearby.

'Hoy! You two! Bugger off!'

They look up, give him the finger, saunter on. The window slams back down. I cross the road, stay close to the wall. I'm on the wrong side of the street now and I daren't go any nearer the little house. The noise from the black guys will have attracted attention from more people than just the old man in the upstairs window. I stay put for a few moments, let the black guys get well past, then look back at the house. All seems quiet. No change at all since the man first went in there. I dip my head, walk slowly down towards it, then stop, check the number. OK, twenty-four Silverton Road.

One place I know they go.

CHAPTER 25

But that's the only thing that's certain. I check out last night's addresses and they don't exist either. I don't see the slimy guys, or the woman from the shadows, and I'm glad of that. I was worried I might. But the streets are deserted. So is Hunter's Moon. No lights, no voices, no music, a *For Sale* sign high up on the wall. Was that there before? I don't remember seeing it, but it was dark and I was scared and looking for other things, so maybe I never noticed it.

Either way, there's nothing happening there. I stay well back, checking from the other side of the street. The place still feels dangerous, and suddenly I'm thinking about tonight and I'm frightened all over again, and I'm running because there's somewhere I desperately want to be.

* * *

They're nice to me at the hospital. They're really nice. They make me tea, they give me biscuits, someone brings me a sandwich and a slice of cake, they sit me down and make a fuss of me, and tell me Mum's doing fine. But they won't let me talk to her. Because she's sleeping and she badly needs to rest.

'Can't I just look at her?'

One of the nurses takes me through and I stand there and gaze down at the sleeping figure in the bed. She doesn't look any better than last time, but I guess the doctors know what they're talking about. Funny thing, though. She looks wasted and yet she's still . . . I don't know . . .

'She looks beautiful,' I say.

Don't know why I'm saying this to the nurse. It's only going to embarrass her. But she answers.

'She does, doesn't she? Really beautiful.'

I look round. I've forgotten the woman's name and she's told me at least twice.

'You'll soon have her home again,' she says. 'But we'd best leave her now. You don't want her to wake up.'

Yes, I do. I want her to wake up so much. I want her to open her eyes and see me and talk to me and say she loves me.

'I love you, Mum,' I mutter.

I feel the nurse's hand on my arm and look round at her again.

'She loves that book you brought her,' she says.

I see it on the cabinet by the bed.

'Beautiful pictures,' says the nurse. 'She showed me some of them.'

'Did you see the one with the osprey?'

'Yes,' says the nurse, 'and the one with the two king-fishers. I don't know how the cameraman caught them so cleverly.'

'It was a woman took that photo. Got her name under it. Madeleine Brightwell.'

'You obviously spend a lot of time with the book,' says

the nurse, 'and I don't blame you. It's something to cherish.'

I stare at her, unsure how to say what I want. She smiles suddenly and pulls me into a hug.

'It's all right, Zinny,' she says quietly, 'I understand.'

I wish she didn't because I'm crying now and I can't stop. It's not sobbing, it's just stupid whimpery tears, my body shuddering with them. The nurse goes on holding me, murmuring stuff I can't make out. I mumble back at her.

'What did you say your name was?'

'Phaedre.'

No wonder I keep forgetting it. She eases me gently away.

'All right, Zinny?'

'Yeah, thanks.'

'You're doing so well,' she says. 'I know this must be really hard for you.'

She leads me out of Mum's ward and back down the corridor.

'Are you going back to school now, Zinny?'

'Yeah.'

No point telling the truth.

'How did you get here?' she says.

'I walked.'

'Do you want me to arrange a lift for you?'

'Dad's picking me up.'

'How is your dad?'

'OK.'

Phaedre puts a hand on my shoulder.

'I'll walk to the car park with you,' she says.

'He won't be there.'

'You said he was picking you up.'

'Down at the shops.'

Phaedre stops outside the lift and turns to face me.

'Take care of yourself, Zinny. All right?'

I look back at her. She doesn't believe a word I just said. I know it. But she hasn't ticked me off. I want her to hug me again, but I know she won't.

'Thanks, Phaedre,' I say.

She says nothing, just presses the button for the lift and stands there, watching my face. The lift arrives, door opens, no one inside. Phaedre smiles.

'I won't come down with you,' she says. 'I know you can manage.'

I step into the lift and turn to look at her again.

'Can you manage?' she says suddenly.

I can manage a smile, but that's all. The lift door closes and Phaedre disappears from view. I press the button for the ground floor and wait. There's a judder and the lift moves down, and a few moments later I'm out in the car park. The rain's stopped but the sky's still grey and overcast. I walk out to the main road and cut right towards the shops. Five minutes later I'm standing outside the bakery. I pull out my mobile and switch it on. No texts but a voicemail from Mr Latham.

'Zinny, I'm extremely concerned that you came into school this morning and then went off by yourself without telling anyone. You're not in trouble but I'm very anxious to know where you are and if you're all right, so please ring me as soon as you get this message. I'll give you the number for my direct line and also the one for my secretary.'

135

I switch off the mobile, switch it on again, punch in Dad's number. Voicemail, as expected. I want to shout the message but I keep it calm, somehow.

'You said you're going to be late. How late? Can you ring or text me?'

I hang up, stare round at the traffic racing past the shops, look down at the phone again, find the number. I've never rung this one before, never needed to. He always used to answer his mobile. I key it in, wait.

'Billington Watts Delivery Service?' says a woman.

'It's Zinny Okoro here.'

'Yes?'

She doesn't sound interested, but I push on.

'Can you . . . can you tell me where my dad is at the moment?'

Silence.

'Hello?' I say.

More silence, then she answers.

'Can you wait a second?'

'OK.'

The second's at least two minutes and when she does come back, it's only to say she's putting me through to Mr Bradbury. I've heard the name. Dad's mentioned him. Someone important. Only he doesn't sound important when he comes on the phone. He sounds bored, like the woman did. But at least he doesn't waste any more of my time.

'I've no idea where your father is,' he says. 'I sacked him three months ago.'

CHAPTER 26

I go from pub to pub. Bloody Dad. I've got to find the bastard. Maybe he's driving, maybe he's miles away. He probably is. But I don't know what else to do. I want to find him and hit him and tell him what I think of him, and then hit him again. He never told us, never had the spine. Well, he never told me. Maybe Mum knew, but I don't reckon she did. She'd have said something about it.

What worries me is what we've been living off. We've never had much money anyway, but three months with no wages from Dad, and yet he had stuff in his wallet, a bit anyway. I saw it. Or maybe it was just Mum paying for the important things. But her wages are worse than what he used to bring back, so that doesn't make much sense. I got nothing from Mr Bradbury.

'Why did you sack my dad?'

'Ask him yourself.'

Down with the phone.

He's not in any of the pubs I try. No surprise there. Don't know why I'm bothering really. I look in the ones I know he likes, and the betting shops, but he's nowhere to be seen, and I'm getting tired and hungry now, and scared again about tonight. But I can't go home yet. I'm frightened of the house too now, and I don't want to be there on my own, and one thing's certain: I won't find Dad waiting there for me. Christ knows what time he's going to show up tonight. I check his last text again.

Gonna b late

'Whatever that means,' I mutter.

I stare round me at the cars and taxis and buses rumbling by, the faces in the moving traffic: lives hurrying past, people I'll never see again. They don't check me out and why should they? Nobody does, not even the passers-by on the pavement. I don't have a story or anything they might want to stop for. I don't have a mum who's been shot or a dad who's a drunk. I'm just some kid standing outside a betting shop. I wander down to the traffic lights, turn left in the direction of Abbot Street, and then stop. There's a car pulling up down Bicton Lane and I recognize it.

Oily Coily's.

What the hell's he doing up here? We're some way from Abbot Street. But I can guess. One of his other properties. He wouldn't live in a road like this one. The houses are too run down. But they're the kinds of places he rents out. I should know. Even our house looks better than some of these, and that's saying something. But why's he just stopped there? I keep out of sight, behind a phone box, and peer round. Definitely Mr Coily's car. I've seen it enough times, and there's Oily himself, in the driver's seat. I can just make out the shape of his head from behind. But he's not alone in the car. There's more heads I can see, two guys in the back, and another in the front.

Got to be careful. They could spot me easily in the wing mirrors if I don't watch out. Not quite sure why this matters. I shouldn't have to worry. Coily's other business is nothing to do with me and he's already given me his nasty little threat that time in the kitchen. I don't suppose he needs to give it again, so there's no reason why I can't just walk on past. But I stay where I am, and now I'm glad, because three of the car doors are opening. Not Coily's. He stays in the driver's seat. But suddenly there's three guys out in the road.

Rough-looking men, thirties, and I'm starting to understand what they're here for. They don't hurry but just walk confidently in through the gate of number twelve and up to the door. Guy in front looks like the leader, though he's not the man in charge. The man in charge is still sitting in the car. Don't think he's even watching them. I haven't seen his head turn to the right. I see the leader guy ring the doorbell, then the three of them wait. Coily's head stays like it was, not moving.

No one answers the door. Somehow I'm not surprised, but I can see two windows open upstairs, and I'm not sure I didn't spot a shadow moving there a moment ago, and if I did, probably those guys did too. I know what they're here for now, and I know what Dad's in for, or Mum, or me, if I'm alone in the house when they come. One of them's pulled out a mobile. He punches in a number, stands back from the front door and gazes up at the open windows, the phone to his ear. I see him start talking, calm and easy, like they all are, for the moment.

I wonder if he's got through. Maybe he's just talking to an answerphone. But even if he is, someone's heard him, because a few moments later, the front door opens.

And the men walk in.

I turn and run back the way I came. Don't care if Coily sees me in his wing mirror. I've got to get away from here, even if it's only into bigger trouble, which I know it will be. I reach the top of Bicton Lane and my mobile rings. I stop, pull it out. It's the school number. It'll be Mr Latham trying me again. I let it ring and run round the block to the next road that heads in the direction of Abbot Street. I hear the phone stop as Voicemail kicks in. Feel guilty not answering, because I know Mr Latham means well, but it's no good. I can't face him. If he gets involved in any of this, the police'll get involved too, and that's the end of it for Mum. It'll be the end for Dad too, but I'm not sure how much I care about him any more.

An hour later I'm at the top of Abbot Street, but I'm not ready to try the house. I'm still too scared of it. I wander down just far enough to see if there's anyone parked outside our place. No sign of Dad's van, of course. Couple of cars I don't recognize, crappy old things, so they're probably nothing to worry about. Certainly no sign of Coily's car, or Flash Coat's. I'm not going further, though. I'm spending as little time as possible in our house right now.

I head back to the top of Abbot Street, cut down behind the fish and chip shop, then slump against the wall by the bins and wait, out of sight of the road. Darkness falls and I drift into sleep, and somehow—of all the weird things—find myself dreaming about running: not running for Flash Coat and his bastard heavies, but on the track, last year, when I won all those medals for my school, and Mr Latham was so pleased with me. Feels good for a bit, but then I wake up again with hunger grinding in my stomach and the smell from the fish and chip shop driving me crazy. It's half past seven at night and I can't put it off any longer. I struggle to my feet and head for home.

CHAPTER 27

The house has been burgled again. I can tell the moment I walk in. It's not a mess, but they haven't tried to hide they've been here either. Stuff clearly moved and left lying about. I try for the millionth time to work out what this mystery thing is that Flash Coat wants so much. But it's no good. I can't guess it and I'm certainly not looking for the bloody thing any more. If they haven't found it with all their rummaging, I certainly won't. But maybe they got it this time. Maybe they'll leave us alone now. Somehow I don't think that's going to happen, and I can't act like it is. Got to see things through tonight, till they tell me to stop. If they ever do.

Dad's not here. Of course.

I pull out my mobile, listen to the message from Mr Latham. Pretty much like the last one: kind, worried, wants me to ring him, which I can't do. Then I hear a ping, and it's a text from Dad.

Dunno wen bak

'Yeah, mate,' I mutter. 'Like you think I don't get it.'

Only I do get it. He's not coming back, not at all, not ever. I know it. He's clearing out for good and he hasn't

142

even got the bottle to tell me straight. All I get is this.

'Dunno when back. Yeah, you bastard.'

Maybe Bradbury phoned him after I phoned him and said your kid's just rung and I told him I sacked you. Maybe you should have told him yourself blah blah blah. Or maybe he's just thinking of Mr Coily and his threat. Who cares? He's gone and that's it.

'Spineless git,' I go on. 'Mum's been shot and I'm in the shit and all you're doing is walking out on us.'

I stare about me. The house seems so quiet. I walk upstairs, down again, into the kitchen, back into the hall, stand there, thinking. Upstairs again, into my room, throw myself on the bed. I'm not going to cry this time, not going to let myself. I was weak with that nurse. She was kind, she was really kind, and I've forgotten her name yet again, but the thought of her kicks me off, and I'm crying in spite of myself, not whimpery tears this time but big, sobby ones. They're just pouring out of me and I let them. I've stopped feeling angry with myself. I'm too angry with Dad.

When the tears finally stop, I find even that's gone: the anger. I lie there, thinking of Dad and wishing the rage would come back, but it's gone with the tears. I just feel sorry for him now. I don't reckon he deserves that, but it's how I feel. I sit up, slide off the bed, walk through to Mum and Dad's room, look round. They came in here too, the burglars, but they don't seem to have moved much. Maybe they reckon they checked it properly last time. Or the time before. Or however many times they've been in here.

I've stopped caring.

I walk downstairs, into the kitchen, hunt for some food. Couple of duff apples in the bowl. They look as grotty as the one Dad gave me. I take one through to the front room, slump on the sofa. Still the silence. Feels weird, because this house has never felt silent, not really silent. There's always the hum of the city close by, except when I look at the photos in that book. Then it's quiet. Then I can pretend I'm somewhere else. But I haven't got the book here, and somehow I don't think I can pretend without it, not very well anyway.

I eat the apple, close my eyes, and to my surprise find I can pretend after all. I see the picture of those king-fishers in my head, and the ponies on Dartmoor, and the moon over Coniston, and the salmon leaping up the river, and that one of the adder I always skip. I picture myself running again, not on the track this time with Mr Latham cheering me on, but round the lake, over the high fells, under the night sky.

But I can't pretend for long because I'm too scared about tonight. The hunger's ripping through me too. I open my eyes. The house is dark, apart from a smoky light from the street lamp pushing through the windows. I'm curled up on the sofa, the apple core squashed inside my right hand. My body's aching all over. Something creaks somewhere in the house. I sit up on the sofa.

'Dad?' I call.

All stays quiet. I stand up, walk through to the kitchen, drop the apple core in the bin. I don't want to put the lights on. I check the time again. Nine o'clock. Not long before I have to go. I poke round for food again. Can't face that last apple in the bowl. Both the ones I've had tasted crap. I think of the fish and chip shop and feel inside my pockets for some money. Pointless: I know there's nothing in them. I wander round the house, aimlessly opening drawers, and to my surprise find some odds and sods of loose change, not enough for what I'd like to have but maybe I'll get lucky if I'm polite. I hurry out of the house and up to the fish and chip shop at the top of Abbot Street. Rashid wants to see my money first.

'Not enough there for fish and chips, boy,' he says.

'Can't you do me a small piece of fish?'

'No, boy.'

'Half a piece?'

'Fish or chips, boy. Can't have both. Not without you get some more money.'

'Give me a break, Rashid.'

'Look over there, boy.' He nods to the price chart on the wall. 'Clear as day. So you give me a break instead, OK? My prices are low already. Fish or chips?'

'Chips.'

'Good boy.'

He holds out his hand for the money. I give it to him with a scowl. He scoops me the chips, wraps them up, hands them over.

'See you around, boy,' he says.

I've eaten the chips by the time I reach home. The house is still dark but I step inside anyway and listen to the silence. I wasn't expecting Dad to be back, wasn't hoping either. I've given up hoping where he's concerned. I stuff the greasy wrapping paper in the bin and glance at my watch again. No point taking my jacket off.

It's time to go. I picture the place with no address, then step out of the house again and into Abbot Street.

I'm seeing shadows everywhere now, some moving, some still. Don't know if they're real or in my head. I set off towards the railway bridge, cut round to the left and on past Ashgrove Park. It's dry but it's cold and my breath feels heavy on the night air. Past the shopping arcade, over the pedestrian precinct. I wish I could take a bus but that's all my money gone. Half an hour later and the streets are still crowded and there are plenty of people hanging round City Stadium. I check my watch again.

Ten minutes to midnight. I'm not going to be late, but that's the only certain thing about the next few minutes. I walk on past the dodgy cafes and bars. Nobody stops me or calls out, but I'm getting noticed, like I was before. Mostly guys but women too, a kind I recognize. I cut down Silverton Road, walking slowly. No lights on at number twenty-four. I carry on past and on towards the T-junction where number eighty-nine would be, if it existed. My watch says midnight and there's a figure standing on the pavement, blocking my way.

'Hey, tadpole,' it says.

CHAPTER 28

I stare. Spink's the last person I was expecting to find waiting for me here. He looks even more terrified than he did at school today, and in a weird kind of way I think he's pleased to see me. Maybe now he's getting bullied himself for the first time in his life he's got an idea of what I've been going through with him. He's certainly not looking at me like I'm fist fodder any more, if anything, the opposite: an ally, a mate, even. He doesn't bother with small talk, just nods me towards the alleyway I hid in earlier. I follow him off the street and into the shadows.

'Now, listen,' he mutters, glancing past me at the road, 'you got to move fast tonight.'

'Why?'

'Cos you got five deliveries and we got to be done by three or we're in the shit.'

'We?'

'We're working together tonight,' he says. 'I give you the packages, you deliver 'em.'

I hold out my hand. He reaches inside his coat, pulls out a package.

'What about the others?' I say.

He shakes his head.

'You don't get more than one at a time. That's what they told me. So you got to really shift. Just hand it over and get back here quick to collect the next one.'

'And there's five of them?'

'Yeah.'

'Are all the addresses near here?'

'Christ knows,' he says. 'I only got given the next address. And listen—if I'm not here any time you get back, you wait, OK? You don't just piss off.'

I take the package and shove it inside my belt, then zip my jacket up over it, and look at Spink's face again: his petrified face. I wonder where the bullyboy went, and it makes me try my luck.

'What's in these packages?'

'Dunno,' says Spink.

'You must have an idea.'

'They don't tell me and I don't ask. And you shouldn't neither.'

But I don't need to ask any more. I've already guessed it's drugs. I just wanted to hear Spink say it. He catches my arm suddenly.

'Listen, mate,' he says.

I look at him. 'Mate' isn't the kind of word Spink's ever used before. Not with me anyway. He glances up the alleyway, then back at me.

'Run fast tonight, Zinny, OK?'

'I'm going to.'

'I mean really fast. I need you to. Cos I'm in a bit of trouble.'

148

'What do you mean?'

'They're not happy with me.'

'Who? Flash Coat?'

'Yeah, and the others.' Spink glances towards the street again. 'I've screwed up a couple of times and they don't like it. So this is my last chance tonight.'

He looks back at me.

'So do your best, Zinny, OK? Fast as you can. I won't forget it.'

'OK.'

'Stand by me and I'll stand by you.'

I can't believe I actually feel sorry for him, but there's no time to talk about that now.

'Where do I take the package?' I say.

He tells me and I'm gone. Least it's not far. I don't get to the address of course, but I never expected to. I'm stopped by a black guy who walks out of a side street, watches me go past, then calls my name. I stop and look back at him. Dreadlocks, bling, mid-twenties. He makes a click in his cheek like he's coaxing a horse. I stay where I am.

He makes the noise again, holds out his hand. I look round. Dark little street, high walls, houses well back, not much in the way of traffic or people. We're not alone, though. Feels public enough to be scary. But I haven't got time to be scared, and the black guy's in a hurry too.

'Give it, boy,' he snaps.

I walk over, give him the package and he turns back down the side street and disappears. I find Spink still in the alleyway, only further down than last time, and more jittery than ever. He beckons me with a jerk of his arm.

'Quick!' he calls.

I hurry over to him. He looks right on the edge now, ready to fall apart, if he hasn't already done so, and he's breathing hard, like he's been running too.

'You took ages,' he growls.

'I couldn't have run any faster.'

'OK, OK.'

He thrusts another package into my hand.

'Do this one quicker, all right?'

'Where's it going?'

He gives me the address and shoves me back towards the street. This one's further, a little mews behind a block of flats. I'm almost there when a figure climbs out of a parked car just in front of me. Big guy, cropped hair, older than the one with dreads. I see the shadow of another guy inside the car. Clunk of a door and he gets out too, smaller, chunkier, same cropped hair. They don't move. They just block the way to the back of the flats.

'What you got, boy?' says the big guy.

I catch a movement deep in the shadows behind them among the bins at the bottom of the flats, then all's still again. I check the big guy again.

'What you looking for?' I say.

'Everything you got, honeyface.'

I turn and run back the way I came. For a few moments I hear footsteps behind me, but then they stop and all I catch is laughter. I keep on running to the end of the street, then check round. No sign of the two guys. I wait a few minutes, then creep back. The car's still there but no one's in it. I glance round and there's the movement by the bins again, and now a new figure's coming forward. Oriental-looking guy. He calls my name, like it's to reassure me, but that's all he says. He just takes the package and runs off, and I do the same. Spink's out of his mind by the time I get back to the alleyway.

'What the hell happened to you?'

'There were these two guys,' I say. 'They came after me. I had to shake them off and go back.'

But he's not listening.

'Take this and run like shit,' he says. 'You got time to make up.'

He slams another package into my hand, gabbles the address and kicks me back out of the alleyway. Least this should be quick. Other end of City Stadium, little side street running down to the main road—but I'm in trouble well before then. I'm not even out of Silverton Road and there's figures spreading across the road to block me. I stop, glance at number twenty-four. It's just down the street on the other side and all dark.

But even if there were lights on and faces looking out, I know they wouldn't help me. They'd just punish me for getting caught. I turn and sprint back the other way. Can't help glancing down the alleyway as I pass. No sign of Spink. He must have nipped off quick after kicking me out. I reach the end of Silverton Road, cut left, left again and round the block back to the stadium. I don't check to see if the figures are still there, just cross the road, jinking between taxis, and run down to the side street Spink told me about.

Waddell Road, easy enough to find. Grotty little lane with broken glass all over the place, like there's just been a gang fight. I think of the number Spink gave me, check the nearest house, and give a start. It's this one: number thirteen. I never expected it to exist. Then I see that the building's empty: broken down, walls crumbling, roof falling in. A hand grabs my shoulder from behind and a voice whispers in my ear.

'Number thirteen. Unlucky you.'

CHAPTER 29

The hand whirls me round and there's two Asian-looking guys standing there, early twenties, but I don't get to take in much more. I feel a thump in my chest and I'm flying backwards into the middle of the street. I land with a jolt among the broken glass, shards grazing my skin, the breath smashed from me. The two guys step towards me.

I start to scramble to my feet but I'm only half-up when I feel their hands lock round my arms and under my thighs, and now they've lifted me, and they're driving me towards the gate of number thirteen. A moment later it crashes into me, and I'm dropped to the ground again. I stare up, dazed. They're standing over me, leering, one guy leaning on the open gate.

'Bit late to be out, kid,' he says.

'Specially if you got something juicy,' says the other, 'cos we might have to lighten your load.'

They don't get a chance. I see something move in the gateway of number thirteen, something dark coming from the empty house, then hear a sick thud and the guy who was leaning in the opening goes tumbling back-

153

wards. The dark thing follows him and a second dark thing takes its place.

Two men, hard bastards. The one in the street's already kicking the shit out of the guy on the ground. The other mugger turns and legs it. The man in the gateway watches his mate for a moment, like it's all normal, like the whimpering and the blood aren't there. I can't look. I just peer up at the man's face, waiting for the same thing to happen to me. He turns at last and stares down at me.

'Scum, these muggers,' he says in a conversational voice. The whimpering has stopped now but the thuds go on. 'Wouldn't have happened, though, if you'd turned up on time.'

He holds out his hand. I give him the package. He takes it, looks it over for a moment, then turns his eyes back on me.

'Don't be late next time,' he says. 'You got that, boy?'

I want to say yes, whatever you want, but I can't speak. His face hardens and I feel the words rush out.

'Yeah, mister. I got it.'

He goes on staring down at me. His mate comes over and joins him. I can't look at the man's face. I just sense it, like I sense the body twitching among the broken glass. The men don't even glance at it as they walk off. I wait till they've gone and then I'm running again, but not to City Stadium, not to Silverton Road, not to the alleyway. I'm racing for home, even though it's not home, even though there's no one there and it'll mean trouble for me tomorrow when they come looking for me.

And then I remember Mum, and what they said they'll do to her, and Dad, weak, spineless Dad who's run away, because they'll track him down too, I know they will, and whatever else I think of him, however much I pretend I don't care about him, I don't really want him beaten up and killed; and then I think of Mum again, and stop in front of Central Library.

Two in the morning. Five deliveries by three, Spink said, or we're both in the shit. But we're in the shit already. I turn back, running hard again. Seems pointless. I won't make the rest of the deliveries and the last guy made it clear he wasn't happy being kept waiting. Whoever's next'll be even less happy, and it'll only get worse as the night goes on, but I've got Mum's face in my mind, and stupid Dad's, and I'm tearing back through the streets, still fizzing with people round the clubs and bars.

Here's Silverton Road again. I don't worry about the figures I saw earlier. Some of them are still hanging round but I pelt between them, past number twenty-four, still dark and gloomy and seemingly deserted, and on to the alleyway. Spink's not there. I check round, then back down the alleyway. He told me to wait here if he's not back. I don't want to but I walk in.

Smell of piss. That wasn't here before. I go right down the alleyway to the wall at the end. More piss. I can see it too now, even in the darkness. I think of Spink again, look back towards the street. This is a bad place to wait. Anyone can block me in from the other end. I walk back, see a figure stop in the opening, sideways on. Big guy, lighting a cigarette, not looking this way yet.

I keep still, stay in the dark best I can. Don't know if he'll see me if he turns this way. I'm hoping I'm far enough down to stay hidden. He moves on suddenly, and I breathe out. Moment later a police car drives past the opening and disappears. Twenty more minutes and still no sign of Spink. I creep to the opening and peer round into the street. There's a car outside number twenty-four, a familiar car. Nobody in it and the house still looks dark. Then a figure appears in the doorway.

Flash Coat.

Even from here and with no street light over him he looks groomed and perfect. He's talking on his phone, cool and calm like he always is. I'm getting more scared by the second. Whatever else is going on with Spink, Flash Coat'll know by now that we're behind with the deliveries and we're not going to get done by three. And I'm sure I've seen his head turn at least once in this direction.

I crouch as low as I can, sneak round into Silverton Road and up the pavement towards the T-junction at the end, then slip behind a parked car and peer down again towards number twenty-four. I can just see it from here, and Flash Coat's no longer standing in the entrance. He's heading towards the alleyway, still talking on his phone. I can see his eyes moving now. They're flicking round, like they're searching, but not for danger. What danger could there possibly be for a guy like this? I don't suppose he's ever felt fear in his life.

He stops outside the alleyway, and peers down. I want to run now, before he comes up this end of the street or sends his men up, but I don't dare move yet because I know he'll see me. I've got to choose the right moment. It's about running now, whatever the consequences. Flash Coat hasn't come for a chat, and now there's more movement down the street, three figures coming out of the doorway of number twenty-four, men I recognize from the first time Flash Coat came after me.

They pile into the car, one of them also on a mobile, and now the engine's purring its familiar song, and they're pulling out, and Flash Coat's walking back to meet them. Now's the moment. I dash towards the T-junction, trying to keep the parked car between me and them, but already I can hear the engine revving up. I duck round into the next street and race towards the traffic lights, searching the houses for a door to hide in. They're all too shallow but I dive into the next door I come to and huddle there. From behind me comes the sound of the motor, but then all of a sudden it's past me and gone. I breathe slowly out, take a few minutes to calm down, then set off for home.

Only to find the car waiting there.

CHAPTER 30

It's not outside our house. It's down the bottom of Abbot Street, under the railway bridge. Don't know if they've seen me coming. I'm behind an old van now, hoping they haven't. Only now I'm not even sure they're in the car. Hard to make it out without going closer, and there's no way I'm doing that. I stare, hoping the darkness'll clear a bit. You'd think they'd keep the driver sitting there at least, but I'm sure the car's empty.

Which means only one thing.

I check over the house. All dark, just how I left it. Seems stupid me wanting to go in when there's nothing in there but getting killed. I can picture the men turning the place over. Not Flash Coat probably. He's most likely sitting there as the others do the work. Or maybe no one's doing any work. Maybe it's all about me now. I didn't bring them the thing they want and they haven't found it on their other searches, and now I've let them down, so maybe they're all just sitting there, waiting for the kid to turn up so they can blow his brains over the wall.

Before they go looking for his mum and dad.

I hear the clunk of a car door and stiffen. Someone's got in over there, driver's seat, I think. I watch, close as I can. No sound of the other doors, but then the engine starts up, the headlights go on. I crouch again, keeping close to the old van. The car starts to move towards me. I gauge the moment, watching the beam from behind the van, then slip round the side as the car purrs past.

I keep low, watching as it speeds back to the main road. Didn't get a glimpse of who was in it. Too risky to look. The car's still driving away but who was in it? That's what's bothering me. I don't dare go into the house to find out. I creep into the shadows over to the right and sit down close to the wall. Takes me a few moments to remember this was the place where that guy hid, the one who shot Mum.

I want to move away now, but I stay there, like he did, watching the house. It's still dark and I'm too nervous to go in. An hour later I'm still there, slumped on the pavement. No one's walked by. I never knew Abbot Street could be this quiet. There's been the odd car but no one on the pavement, no one to notice me. I pull out my mobile. No messages. I check my watch: quarter to five. No sign of dawn but I'm hearing more traffic in the city.

I stare at the house again: dark, silent as before. I'm still scared, but I can't stay out here any longer. I look round, look back, walk over the road and up to the front room window. Glance through the gap in the curtains, and gasp. They've ransacked the place, a hundred times worse than before. It's like a hurricane's ripped the room apart. If the rest of the house is like this, I don't think I can bear to look. I walk up to the front door, finger the key in my pocket, then change my mind and slip round to the alleyway behind the gardens, and down to our back door.

It's half-open. My mind spins back to the time Flash Coat picked the lock and crept in while I was inside; and now I'm wondering if everything's reversed, if I'm creeping in the back door and there's someone else already there, listening and waiting. I just hope I'm wrong. I step up to the door, ease it wider, put my head through the gap. No sound from within, but I can already see the devastation.

Everything imaginable's been smashed, thrown down or knocked over, and this wasn't a search. Oh, no. It's got nothing to do with the thing they've been looking for. They've given up on that now. This is revenge, pure and simple, and they'll be coming for me next, and Mum, and Dad. It's over, whatever life we had. We can't beat these people. They're too powerful and even the police won't keep us safe.

I think of Dad again. Deep down I know it's his fault, all this. Whatever's kicked up this storm, it's got something to do with him. All those long drives he won't talk about, all those secrets, and now he's buggered off when we need him most, just set the whole mess going and left me and Mum to deal with it, useless pillock. Not that I want him hurt or anything. I don't want those bastards to get him. Whatever he's done, I don't want that. But I wish I could throttle him myself.

I walk through the downstairs rooms. Everything's chaos—kitchen, hall, front room. There's nobody in this part of the house. I stop at the foot of the stairs and look up. All's quiet above me. I start to climb, listening hard, but all I hear is the city waking up outside, and the silence around me in our broken little house. I reach the top of the stairs and look about me.

Chaos again, even on the landing, the wall clock torn down and smashed, the mirror shattered. Mum and Dad's bedroom has been wrecked; so has mine. They didn't overturn my bed like they did with Mum and Dad's, but the rest of the room's come off just as badly. I walk into the bathroom. They've even smashed up the loo and the bath. There's glass everywhere, with the mirror and cabinet down too. I go back to my room, throw myself on the bed, then pull out my phone again and try Dad's number. Voicemail as usual. I text him.

Why aren't u here?

'You never are, you bastard,' I mutter.

I ring the hospital. A woman answers.

'I want to speak to Mrs Okoro,' I say.

'Mrs Okoro?'

'Mrs Dana Okoro.' I hear my voice rising but I can't stop it. 'She's my mum and she's been shot and you've got her in your hospital and I know she's sleeping and she needs rest and it's early in the morning and you can't wake her, but I'm her son and my dad's gone missing and I'm in trouble and I bloody need her.'

I stop, listen. From the mobile phone comes the sound of the woman talking back. I hang up quick and go on listening. At first all seems quiet, but then I catch it again.

The sound of footsteps downstairs.

CHAPTER 31

Stealthy sounds, not like Flash Coat and his mates must have been when they smashed the place up. These footsteps are cautious. They're moving from room to room downstairs, as though the person's checking no one's here, or maybe just gawping at the destruction. Not staying long, though, not down there. I can hear the steps heading for the stairs, and they're moving faster now, like there's an urgent reason for coming up. I glance down at the bed.

No time to hide under it. I'll get heard wriggling about. All I can do is creep behind the door and brace myself, because the moment that person comes into my bedroom, I'll be clear to see. But the footsteps don't come this way, or to Mum and Dad's bedroom. They head down the landing towards the bathroom and then stop before they get there. Another silence, then a new sound down the landing, the click of a door, and I recognize it. I tiptoe to the edge of my bedroom door and peer round.

I can see the airing cupboard door open, and someone's backside sticking out. Definitely a guy. Can't see much more of him because he's bending into the airing cabinet and fumbling about inside. I can see towels flying out over his shoulder and now there's a crinkling sound like he's ripping something back—and then I get it. He's peeling back the jacket round the immersion tank.

Takes him a few moments and he's reaching right inside now, almost buried in the airing cupboard. Still the ripping sound, like he's tearing away the jacket from the very back of the tank, then the sound stops, and I hear a grunt, a satisfied grunt, and he starts to straighten up. And then he seems to sense something and his head comes back and he sees me for the first time.

And I see him, and I know who he is, because he's twisted his whole body round to face me, and I've seen his cheapjack shoes, the shoes trying to be posh, like the rest of him, only none of it's working. His shirt's cheap, his trousers are cheap, his bling's cheap. He's cheap.

'Romeo,' I mutter.

Funny how I'm not scared of him. He looks back at me, still a bit wary but getting more confident now he's seen it's just a boy. I try to work out what Mum could possibly see in this jerk. Even Dad's got more going for him than this loser. Except Dad's not here. Romeo goes on watching me, one arm still inside the airing cupboard, like he's hiding something.

'You might as well show me,' I say.

'Show you what?'

Smarmy voice. I recognize it from last time.

'Whatever it is you came back here to get,' I say.

He pulls the hidden arm out and he's holding a large brown package. It just like the ones I've been delivering, only much, much bigger. Doesn't look like it's been opened. I can see the staples and tape still in place. I think of Flash Coat and what he'll do to both of us for this package. Romeo's walking over with it now, all smiles.

'Your mum's been hiding this,' he says. Puts a hand on my shoulder. 'I take it you're Zinny?'

I don't answer but I don't need to, because he goes straight on.

'She did a naughty thing, Zinny, I'm afraid. I know it's not something you want to hear about your mum, specially when she's been shot, but it just goes to show how serious this is. She's got herself in deep, Zinny, and she's upset some dangerous people.'

He pauses for a moment, like he's wanting me to smile or say something.

'Can you take your hand off my shoulder?' I mumble.

He doesn't seem to hear this, just leaves it there and goes on.

'We were doing this cleaning job, Zinny. I'm Dana's boss, by the way. Don't know if you knew that. Actually, come to think of it, we spoke on the phone, didn't we? When you rang to tell me about your poor old mum getting shot. Horrible business. I've been really worried about her.'

'Get on with it.'

His face changes for a moment and the smirk disappears, like he's actually surprised I don't seem to like him, then he gives my shoulder a squeeze.

'I understand, Zinny. You don't trust me because you don't know me. But I promise you I'm a friend and I'm just trying to look out for Dana and help her. Because, like I said, she did a naughty thing and that's why she got shot, so you and I have got to work together to keep her safe, all right?'

'What's in the package?'

'Well, Zinny, the thing is,' he says, all matey now, 'I've got no idea. All I know is that Dana told me it's something worth keeping secret. And that's where I started to worry about her. I mean, I know you guys are hard up and struggling to pay the rent and everything, but this is going too far and you've only got to see what's happened to your mum and now this house to agree with me on that one.'

'Get to the point.'

Again the surprised look, like he still can't believe I don't trust him; then he gives a shrug.

'We were cleaning an old pub,' he goes on, 'called Hunter's Moon. It's up for sale and the guy who rang me said he wanted us to give it a good sparkle to impress potential buyers. I sent three of my staff out there, including your mum, and during the morning I went out to check how they were doing. Didn't see anyone from the pub but one of my cleaners said there was a guy somewhere on the premises, so I just checked how the cleaning was going. Two of my people were doing the main area downstairs but there were a few upstairs rooms they wanted done and Dana was on her own up there. I nipped up to see how she was getting on, thought she looked OK, so I went off. Then later that day I got a call from her sounding frightened and saying she wanted to speak to me but not at work. She said you were at school and your dad was out driving somewhere so would I come round here?'

He edges closer, like it's suddenly confidential. I lean

back. Can't bear to listen to this guy any more, but I've got to make myself. I might just be able to pick some of the truth out of his story. If there's any in there.

'To be honest, Zinny,' he goes on, 'I felt a bit uncomfortable about that, you know? There's a professional code when it comes to dealing with staff. Things you just don't do as a manager and meeting in private with a married female employee is one of them. But I could tell Dana was in a state about something so I came round.'

I want to hit him so much now. I just want to slug his face and never stop. I hold back somehow and luckily he ploughs on.

'She showed me this package, all sealed like it is now. I asked her where she got it. She looked guilty, then she told me she took it from Hunter's Moon. Said there was another set of stairs up from the floor where she was cleaning. They'd been told not to go up there, it was out of bounds, but once she'd finished cleaning the upstairs rooms, she couldn't resist having a look. There was no one else around and she just couldn't stop herself. It was an office, she said, and there were loads of these big packages, all sealed and all the same. Loads and loads of them, she said.'

He pauses again, watching me close, then lowers his voice.

'Then she told me she knew what was in them. Because there was one in the pile that wasn't quite sealed properly, so she had a look. And that's when I stopped her, Zinny.'

'Doing what?'

'Telling me what was inside. Because I don't want to know, OK? I've got my integrity to think of.'

'Yeah, right.'

'It's true, Zinny,' he says. 'It's important. Lose your integrity and you lose everything. And what worried me was that your mum might have done just that. But she hadn't. That's the good news. She'd taken one of the packages, thinking no one would ever miss it when there was so many there, and she'd walked out with it. OK, she'd had a moment of madness. But then her good sense kicked in and she realized she'd made a mistake. So she called me. Because she didn't know what to do. So I helped her to hide it, while we decided on the next step. But unfortunately, as you and I both know, they spotted the missing package and came looking for it, and for Dana.'

'How did they find out where she lived?'

'Easy as pie,' says Romeo. 'They'd have remembered which of the cleaners did the upstairs floor, so all they had to do was watch our offices next day when the staff arrived for work, check out Dana, keep a discreet eye on her during the day, then follow her home. Bingo! And you know the rest.'

'So what are you doing back here?'

'I wanted to get that package out of the house so it doesn't compromise Dana. I thought if I could just post it back to the people at Hunter's Moon, it might get her off the hook.'

'No need to post it,' says a voice behind me. 'You can just hand it over.'

Romeo gives a start and stares past my shoulder. I whirl round to see Flash Coat standing there. He smiles and pulls out a gun.

CHAPTER 32

He's been in my bedroom all the time. I try to work it out. My wrecked bedroom with nowhere to hide except . . .

'That's right, boy,' he says. 'I was lying under your bed. Nearly messed up my coat.'

But it still looks immaculate, needless to say. I see the smile widen, the gun motion towards the package.

'I'll take that,' he says to Romeo.

'Listen,' says Romeo, still holding it, 'I hope you don't think this has got anything to do with me. I don't know how much you heard just now—'

'All of it.'

'Then you'll know who's responsible for the theft. It's not me. It's Mrs Okoro and I've just come here to try and straighten things out and—'

That's when I hit him. Can't stop myself, even with Flash Coat standing there with a gun. I lash out with all my strength. I catch Romeo full in the face, a proper punch and it startles him, but he steps quickly back, still clutching the package, then grabs my arm as I swing a second punch and pulls me round in front of him as a shield.

'You bastard!' I yell.

I'm facing Flash Coat and struggling to break free but I twist my head round and scream at Romeo.

'Tell him the truth!'

Romeo tightens his grip, the package pressed hard against me as he locks his arms round mine. I stamp on his feet but it makes no difference. I see Flash Coat watching, quiet and dangerous. The smile's gone and he's stepped closer. I go on screaming at Romeo.

'Tell him what happened!'

'He knows what happened,' says Romeo. 'He's heard it all. He just said.'

'He's lying,' I say to Flash Coat. 'He's been having an affair with my mum. I heard them in the house that day you broke in. She won't know anything about your package because she never took it. He did. When he went to check out Hunter's Moon. He probably hid the package here while she wasn't looking, then had to run off and leave it because he heard my dad coming back or something.'

I'm guessing a lot of this but some of it's making sense because Romeo's squeezing me harder now and it's not just to stop me breaking away—it's to hurt me. I stamp on his foot again, harder, but he still won't let go. Then the phone rings downstairs. It seems to freeze us all, even Flash Coat. The answerphone kicks in and I hear Mum's voice—breathless, weak, worried, but angry too and her words reach us easily upstairs.

'Zinny, answer the phone if you're there! Answer the bloody phone!'

She waits a couple of seconds, then hurries on.

'All right, listen. The moment you get this message, you're to stay where you are, you understand? You're not to go out again. I got your message and I'm discharging myself from the hospital and coming straight home.'

I hear other voices, protesting voices. One of them sounds like the nurse who hugged me. But Mum's comes back over the top of them.

'You're to stay in the house, Zinny! We've just had the police in as well. A boy called Ricky Spink's been found dead and Mr Latham's told them you and this kid have been hanging out together. So you're to stay where you are, you got that? I'm coming home now and the police are on their way too.'

She rings off—and Romeo makes his move. He shoves me at Flash Coat and makes a dash for the stairs, still clutching the package. But he doesn't even make the top step. Flash Coat brushes me aside with his left hand, raises the gun with his right, and fires. Romeo crumples to the ground, blood seeping from his head. He doesn't move again. Flash Coat walks over, looks down at him without much interest, then picks up the package, turns to me, and raises the gun again.

'Sorry, Zinny,' he says, 'no witnesses.'

But something checks him. I stand there, staring back. Flash Coat's as relaxed as ever, his eyes on me, the gun trained on my heart, but he's listening. I listen too, and now I catch the sound of cars approaching down Abbot Street as dawn starts to break outside. All of a sudden Flash Coat moves, but not to shoot.

He wedges the big package—with some difficulty—inside his belt, points the gun at my head, then grabs me by the hair with his left hand and yanks me through to Mum and Dad's bedroom and over to the window. I'm whimpering with the pain and I want to beg him to stop but I keep my mouth shut, somehow. He'll blow my head off if I mess with him. He probably will anyway but right now he's peering out. I can see too, even with my head at an angle.

Two police cars are pulling up outside the house, a third heading down towards the railway bridge. Can't work that one out, but Flash Coat seems to get it because he's already pulling me out of the room and down the stairs to the back door. I'm moaning now, can't stop myself, but he takes no notice and jerks open the door, only to slam it shut again and turn the key in the lock, and now he's dragging me back up the stairs. As we near the top I hear the sound of voices by the back door.

'Police!'

Two figures appear, silhouetted in the glass. Flash Coat fires at them and they duck from view.

'I've got the boy,' he roars, 'and I'll shoot him the moment anyone comes in!'

I'm screaming now.

'Let me go!'

Flash Coat wrestles me to the top of the stairs, kicks Romeo's motionless body to the side, and drives me against the wall.

'You don't scream, boy,' he growls. 'You don't make a sound.'

He locks his left hand over my neck, tips my head back. I feel the point of the gun push between my lips, force my mouth open, slip down my throat. I start to gag but it stays there, and now I'm being thrust back into Mum and Dad's room and over to the window again. I see figures down in the street, police mostly, but neighbours too, and the landlord, and a man walking a dog, the officers trying to keep everyone back. Someone sees us at the window.

'There!'

Flash Coat lets go of my neck, picks up the stool by the dresser, and smashes it through the window, then he forces my head towards the opening in the glass, the gun still rammed into my mouth, and bellows down to the street.

'See what I've got!'

I hear shouts down below but Flash Coat thunders on.

'And see what this kid's going to get if anyone comes in!'

I see a blur now, a mixture of broken glass and sky and figures hurrying back from the house and away down the street, even the police. If anyone was hanging round before, they won't be now they know there's a gun. I've still got it planted down my throat and I'm retching up into it. Flash Coat glares down at me, like I've suddenly become a nuisance rather than a hostage.

'Keep still,' he breathes.

And he stares back down at the road. My eyes spin over it too, even as he jerks my head about, and I see more police cars racing down Abbot Street. There's nobody near the house now, but I can see officers stationed on both sides, and I guess they'll be round the back too. Flash Coat watches them for a moment, then jerks me back from the window, pulls the gun from my mouth, and kicks me over into the far side of the room. I crumple on the floor against the upturned wreckage of Mum and Dad's bed. He steps over and points the gun down at me.

'You stay there, kid,' he mutters. 'You don't say anything, you don't do anything. You understand?'

I don't answer. I try to but all I can do is stare at the gun. He leans down with a roar and smacks it into the side of my face. I give a holler of pain.

'You understand?' he snarls.

'Yeah, mister.'

'Do you?'

'Yeah, mister.'

He raises his arm as if to swing the gun again, then lowers it and glowers at me.

'You stay there, boy,' he says.

And he walks over to the window again and peers out. I watch him, my head pounding. He's keeping to the side, like he doesn't want to give marksmen a target, but he's busy texting even as he checks the street. I hear another engine draw close and stop, further up the road. There's a clunk of a car door, and then a voice:

'I've got to see him!'

It's Mum.

CHAPTER 33

Flash Coat stabs a glance at me.

'Stay where you are, boy. Move a muscle and I'll shoot your mum a second time. And this one'll kill her.'

I stare at him, dimly aware of what he's just said and what it means, but he's already turned back to his texting. I catch Mum's voice again, arguing out in the street, and now a man's voice, a policeman probably, trying to hold her back.

'Let me go!' she shouts.

'Keep back from the house, madam.'

'Let me go!'

She sounds nearer now, too near. Flash Coat looks up from his mobile, raises his gun to the gap in the window, and shoots.

'No!' I yell.

I hear a burst of shouts down in the street but nothing from Mum. I start up from the floor, in spite of what Flash Coat said, but he swings the gun round and aims it at me.

'No point, kid,' he mutters. 'She's finished. Now stay there or you're next.'

I slump back again, fighting the pictures in my head. There's a gabble of voices outside, all crowded together, but I can't hear Mum's among them, and now they're drawing back from the house to the safety further up the road. Maybe they're carrying Mum with them or maybe she's just lying on the pavement. I'm desperate to look out but I don't dare move.

Flash Coat's busy with his mobile again. He sends his text, glances at me again, then stares out of the window, and there's a silence, outside, and in here, just his breathing and mine now, and somehow, in this crazy stillness, I hear a blackbird up on the roof, maybe that same one I heard the day Flash Coat first broke in.

'You bastard,' I say to him.

Don't care what he does to me now. Doesn't matter if Mum's dead. He can go ahead and kill me if he wants. Makes no difference to me any more. He doesn't even look at me.

'You bastard,' I say.

There's a ping in his mobile. The blackbird falls silent. He checks the message, texts something back, glances at me. I try to fix him in the eye.

'Good at killing, aren't you?'

He doesn't answer.

'So why Spink?' I say.

I don't expect a reply, but he shrugs.

'Didn't make his deliveries on time.'

'Neither did I.'

'I know you didn't.'

That's when I know I'm dead. Spink's only copped it before me because he's no use any more, and as soon as

175

Flash Coat's got what he wants from his hostage, I'll get it too. But suddenly I'm cool about that. What's to live for now? I hear another ping in his mobile. He checks the message, then takes a long look outside. I rub the bruise in my face and watch him.

'You won't get away,' I say.

'Shut your mouth.'

'The police'll be waiting all round the house.'

'I said shut your mouth!'

For the first time ever he looks flustered. Yet another ping in his mobile. He checks it, sends a message back, scans the street again. It's still quiet, but not as much as when the blackbird was singing. There's a low murmur further up the road. I guess that's where they're all waiting, the residents anyway. I just hope I'm right about the police being all round the house. Then everything moves fast. Flash Coat's mobile rings, he answers it at once, listens for a moment, then cuts it off, and strides towards me.

'Get up!' he says.

I don't move, and this time it's deliberate.

'I won't get up!'

The gun slams into the side of my face again. I reel with the shock of the blow and for a moment lose vision, but it comes back in time for me to see Flash Coat's other hand grab me by the scruff and yank me to my feet.

'Do as you're told!' he bellows.

And there's the gun thrust against my head. I try to resist, but he's shoving me too fast, out of Mum and Dad's bedroom and onto the landing, and down the stairs to the back door. He stops for a moment to unlock it, then seizes me by the hair and pulls me round in front of him.

'Now listen, boy,' he mutters, 'do as I say and you live. Mess with me and you end up dead like your mum. You got that?'

He doesn't wait for an answer. Maybe he's worked out I don't care any more. I hope so, but I haven't got time to think. He's got the back door open and he's kneed me out in front of him and then pulled me back into his body so I'm a shield again, my head jerked by the hair onto his shoulder, the gun forced down my throat, and we're walking, kind of, me hobbling in front of him, locked against his body, the gun making me gob and my eyes swivelling to glimpse what I can, but with my head at this angle, it's mostly sky.

I see bits of things, though. I see the alley down the back of the houses, faces peering down from the some of the upstairs rooms, then we're past the houses and into the street, and I'm getting a flash of police uniforms left and right, too far away to help, and whirling lights from police cars. I hear the crackle of voices in radios, the sound of distant sirens heading from the other end of Abbot Street, a train rumbling over the railway bridge just a short way down. I feel the gun whipped from my mouth, hear a shot into the air, then Flash Coat's bellowing voice.

'Keep your distance or he's dead!'

Don't know if anyone moves. Can't see. He's jerked my head straight back and my eyes are fixed on the sky again, the gun stuffed down my throat like it was before, and now he's nudging me with his knees towards the kerb of the road. There's no car waiting for us yet. I saw that much when he was firing off the gun, but now I hear it, the familiar engine, only now it's not purring, it's roaring with its full voice, and I know where it's coming from.

It's racing towards us from the other side of the railway bridge. I saw police officers down there, I'm sure I did, in that brief glimpse a moment ago, but if they're trying to block cars, they won't stop this one, and they don't. It tears towards us like a moving scream. I still haven't seen it. I'm squinting at the sky, choking on the gun, and now it's pushing down, deeper and deeper into me, and I'm thinking: this is the moment, this is when the car arrives and he doesn't need me any more. This is when he pulls the trigger—and suddenly I'm not ready. Whatever I thought before, I'm not ready to die.

I reach up and try to grab his hand, the one that's tight round the gun. Like that's going to stop him. It doesn't. The gun stays rammed down my throat, but he hasn't pulled the trigger yet, and he's still bundling me towards the kerb. I hear the moving scream grow louder, and suddenly the car's upon us, and Flash Coat's got his other hand on top of my head, and he's pushing me down, down, the gun still in my throat, and we're both ducking together into the open door of the car.

I feel the gun whipped free, and then a shove, and I'm falling over the back seat, and Flash Coat's dived on top of me, and the door's closed again and the car's racing off. I twist round and stare up into Flash Coat's face, but he's not watching me. He's keeping low but he's peering out of the windows as we tear off.

I lift myself up a bit. He waves the gun at me and I freeze, but I'm high enough to see out. Just one other guy in the car and that's the driver, same one as before, and he's belting it. Up to the old garages, police officers running after us, then a yank of the wheel and he's spun us round and we're shooting back towards the railway bridge. The officers break apart left and right and we race on.

I check both directions. He won't head up Abbot Street—too many cars and they'll have blocked the road—so it's got to be the railway bridge. But already I can see police cars pulling across. There's still a gap to the far left and the driver's heading for it. Again I see officers diving for cover. A crash as we pile into a parked police motorbike, then we're shooting through the gap.

The left side of the car squeals as the arch of the railway bridge tears into it. I see the faces of two police-women peering at me from inside the nearest car, and then we're past the roadblock and racing towards the roundabout. Flash Coat straightens suddenly and looks at me; and there's something in his face that needs no words. But he gives me some anyway.

'Sorry, boy,' he says. 'Time to part company.'

He raises the gun; and that's all I remember.

CHAPTER 34

Then some time later I see faces. They kind of freak me out. They're blurred and scary and I don't like them at all. Got no idea who they are. But after a while they stop being scary—I don't know why—and just become boring. I stare at them for a bit and they eventually go away. But they don't go very far, because the next time I look, they're still there; and then one of them speaks.

'Zinny.'

Some woman.

'Twenty-four Silverton Road,' I mumble.

'Zinny,' she says again.

'Twenty-four Silverton Road.'

'We know about twenty-four Silverton Road,' says another voice.

A guy this time. I peer round at the blurry faces. He's over to the left, judging from the voice. Don't know which one the woman is. There's two next to each other, I think. One leans forward suddenly and speaks, and it's the same woman as before.

'Zinny, it's Mum.'

I feel something touch me.

'Zinny, sweetheart.'

'You're dead.'

'No, I'm not.'

'You got shot.'

'He missed, sweetheart.'

I don't answer. Got no words, none at all, just a weird feeling that everything's not real, that this can't be right. No one seems to mind. They just wait, these silent faces; but I feel Mum's hand reach round and find mine, and squeeze it, and then I know it's right. I say something at last.

'Am I dying?'

'Course not, you silly thing.'

She chuckles. Makes me feel a bit better. She always had a good chuckle. I stare round, wishing I could see the faces better.

'You're all blurred,' I say.

'Give it time,' says another voice.

I recognize this one straight off. I even remember the woman's name.

'Phaedre,' I say.

The nurse laughs. She's got a good chuckle too.

'You finally remembered my name,' she says.

'Don't expect me to know it tomorrow.'

She laughs again.

'Am I in hospital?' I say.

'Yes, Zinny,' she says. 'You've had an accident but you're going to be fine. You've been out for some time and you're badly concussed. You've also broken your left arm and some ribs. But you're doing great and you'll soon be able to see us. Your vision's just a bit cloudy, that's all.'

I stare at the other faces. They're still fuzzy, but Phaedre's right. I'm starting to see a bit better. The guy who spoke about Silverton Road's a policeman. He's got another officer next to him—no, wait a minute, it's not an officer, it's some other guy. He speaks.

'It's me, Zinny.'

'Mr Latham?'

'That's right, lad. Well done.'

I feel another hand touch me, and I know it's his.

'Is Spink really dead?' I say.

'I'm afraid so, Zinny.'

'What happened?'

'This isn't the time to talk. You need your rest.'

'I want to know.'

'Better let DI James tell you about it,' says Mr Latham. 'I'm not sure how much I'm allowed to say.'

The police officer speaks without further prompting.

'We found Ricky Spink in an alleyway,' he says, 'but I'm afraid we were too late.'

'How did he—'

'He was shot.'

I take a long breath. It hurts me. Talking hurts too. I didn't expect that. But maybe it's what we're talking about that hurts.

'Can you tell me any more?' I say.

'He rang us in a panic in the early hours of this morning,' says the officer. 'Said he was running for his life, and it sounded like it. He told us about these packages being delivered round the city and said something was going on at twenty-four Silverton Road but he didn't know what it was.'

'Did he say anything about me?'

'Not a word,' says the officer. 'It was only when we spoke to Mr Latham later this morning that we found out that the two of you have been hanging out recently. But by then the boy was dead.'

'Maybe he was trying to protect Zinny,' says Mum.

'It doesn't fit his character,' says the officer, 'and we knew the boy pretty well.'

'Maybe it does fit his character,' says Mr Latham, 'and we didn't know him anywhere near as well as we thought.'

The policeman doesn't answer this. I picture Spink's face, those tiny little eyes that used to mock me as he beat the shit out of me. I think of how much I wanted him dead, and I did once, I really did, only now I want to bring him back, because I've also seen Spink's face when he wasn't mocking me. I've seen it when he was terrified, and I've got a feeling Mr Latham's right and the policeman's wrong. But there's no point talking about that now.

'What about the drugs?' I say.

'Drugs?' says the officer.

'In the packages.'

'It wasn't drugs in the packages.'

I stare at the guy's face, still cloudy like the others. I wish it would clear so I could read his expression. He speaks again.

'It was counterfeit money in the packages.'

'You serious?'

'Yes,' says the officer. 'It's a huge racket and we've known about it for some time, but we haven't been able to trace the source. They print the stuff at a secret location somewhere in the city and just when we get a tip-off and start closing in, they move somewhere else. They were using an old pub for a while—'

'Hunter's Moon.'

'Yes,' says the officer, 'and now obviously Silverton Road. They print off the counterfeit money in huge quantities and the notes are of very high quality indeed. But having printed the stuff off, they then have to feed the bills into the system, and for that they need help.'

I feel Mum squeeze my hand. I squeeze hers back. Wish I could see her face. It's clearer than it was, but I still can't make it out very well, and I'm desperate to see her properly. The policeman goes on.

'It's a very well-organized business. They have people all over the city who cash in the counterfeit notes, usually by buying something very, very small and then pocketing the change, which of course is in legal tender. These people then take their agreed cut of this legal tender and return the rest—which is most of it—to the racketeers.'

'So is that what Zinny's been doing?' says Mum.

'Well, I haven't had a chance to speak to Zinny yet,' says the officer, 'but if he was doing what Ricky Spink was doing, then he was a runner. Is that right, Zinny?'

'I guess.'

'What did you have to do?'

'Go to these different places and deliver little packages. They didn't tell me what was in them and warned me not to look, or else.'

'Did they pay you to deliver these packages or force you?'

'They forced me.'

I'm not telling him what threat they used. But he doesn't ask anyway.

'Ricky Spink told us he got a small cut to begin with,' says the officer, 'but then the money stopped.'

'Why?' says Mr Latham.

'He didn't say, but they must have had something on him because he carried on delivering the packages. He was obviously scared out of his wits by the end.'

'But what do these runners do?' says Mum.

'They deliver the counterfeit money to the agreed receivers around the city,' says the policeman. 'Zinny and Ricky Spink will only have been two runners out of many. The packages contain just enough cash to make the receiver's work worth the risk, but not enough to be a disaster if the runner gets into trouble and the stuff goes missing.'

'What's to stop the receivers keeping the whole consignment?' says Mr Latham.

'If you knew the men behind this racket,' says the officer, 'you wouldn't ask that question, sir. They're extremely dangerous individuals and they see revenge as a matter of honour. People who cross them or fail to do as they're told come to a bad end. You only have to remember what's happened to young Spink.'

I hear Mum crying.

'It's all right, Mum,' I say.

'It's not all right, Zinny,' she says. 'It's not all right at all.'

She goes on crying for a bit, then I hear her blow her nose and say sorry, to the others, I think. There's an awkward silence.

'So what happens now?' says Phaedre.

'Well,' says DI James, 'we're obviously trying to trace as many people involved in this scam as possible, so we're keen to talk to Zinny in more depth about all this.'

'Does it have to be now?' says Phaedre. 'Or even today? The poor boy's just come round.'

'It doesn't have to be now,' says the officer, with obvious reluctance, 'or I suppose even today.'

'But?' says the nurse.

DI James hesitates.

'I'm sure you'll appreciate that we need to move on this as quickly as possible.'

I feel the officer's voice change direction, back to me.

'So it's up to you, Zinny,' he says. 'No pressure. Do you need a bit more rest or are you ready to have a talk? Tell us what you want.'

I don't know what I want. That's the trouble. I'm not sure about anything right now. But I've got some questions of my own.

'There's something I don't get,' I say.

'What's that?' says DI James.

'The first guy I delivered a package to just gave me another one to deliver to somebody else, a woman. Doesn't make any sense.'

'Yes, it does,' says the officer. 'That first delivery was probably a test, a package with nothing valuable in it so they could see if you did as you were told. The moment you dropped it off, they had their answer, and all the deliveries after that would have been for real.'

'So what's happened to the men?'

'We found nobody at Silverton Road and nothing to incriminate anyone. As for the guys in the car you were in, the driver was killed in the accident.'

'And Flash Coat?'

The policeman gives a quiet laugh.

'Is that what you call him?'

'Yes.'

'We have another name for him. Several, in fact.'

I feel Mum lean closer, crying again.

'He's the one who shot you, Mum,' I say, 'that time you went outside. And he tried a second time, the bastard.'

'But I'm still here, sweetheart,' she says, 'aren't I?'

'What happened to him?' I say to the officer.

'He was injured too, but he's been arrested and he's now being questioned on a murder charge.'

'It's not just Spink who got killed,' I say. 'There's also—'

'We know about the gentleman who was shot in your house,' says the policeman. He pauses. 'Mrs Okoro has given us further information about him.'

I'm not sure what that means, and maybe I don't care; because my eyes are slowly clearing and there's something else to think about, something I haven't noticed till now: another figure sitting by the bed, just behind the others, not moving, not speaking, not wanting to be seen maybe. Only I see him. Yeah, I see him now.

'Dad?' I say.

CHAPTER 35

Mr Latham's the first to get up, and then Phaedre. I get a pat on the head from him and a kiss on the cheek from her, and suddenly they've gone, and it's just me and Mum and Dad, and DI James, who's making it quite clear he's going nowhere. I check out Dad's face again, easy to read now, and about as guilty as he could ever look. He hasn't managed a word yet, but if he's not ready to talk, I am. I turn back to the policeman.

'What do you want to know?'

'Whatever you want to tell me.'

So I tell him everything, in front of Mum and Dad: the whole story, apart from Mum and Romeo having a thing. I reckon Mum's already said something about that, and not just to the policeman. She and Dad have had a talk. I can tell. So whether they've got a future or not, I don't know. He looks haunted, that's for sure, but so does she. Probably I do too. The policeman hears me through to the end without interruption.

'Thank you, Zinny,' he says.

I glare at Dad.

'So are you going to say something now or not?'

He doesn't, but Mum does.

'I still don't understand how one package could make those men do all those horrible things to us, especially Zinny. I mean, one package, when they had so many.'

'As I said earlier, Mrs Okoro,' says DI James, 'these are ruthless men who take revenge very seriously. They'd have come for you if you'd only had a fiver of theirs. But you had an awful lot more than that. The package you had in your house was one of the master packages. These weren't the small ones given to runners like Zinny to deliver round the city with just enough counterfeit money to make the receiver's work worth the risk. These bigger packages contained a whole load more money and they were never meant to be taken out on the street. They were more for storage purposes.'

'So how much cash was there inside the package we had?'

'Let's just say a very large amount,' says the officer, and it's clear he's going no further on that one. He stands up and glances down at me. 'Well done, boy.'

'He doesn't like that,' says Dad.

He takes us all by surprise, speaking suddenly. The officer looks round at him.

'What doesn't he like, Mr Okoro?'

'Being called boy.'

'Oh, I see.' The policeman turns back to me. 'Sorry about that, Zinny. Won't do it again.'

I catch Dad's eye, but he looks away. DI James pats me on the shoulder.

'I think that's enough for now, Zinny. You've been very helpful, and very brave. When you're feeling stronger, we'll be in touch again to do things a little more formally, and I'm afraid you and your parents will have to testify at some point about what's happened. I'm also very sorry about the damage done to your house. I presume most of that's covered by your landlord's insurance, but it's not a nice thing to be going home to.'

He glances at Mum and Dad but they say nothing.

'Well,' he says, 'I'll leave you all to it.'

And he's gone. Silence falls over us like a great big weight. No one seems to want to speak. The ward's empty apart from us and the silence just gets heavier. Mum's still holding my hand, leaning close, but she looks embarrassed now. Dad's leaned back again in his chair, and he's still avoiding my eyes.

'Useless git,' I say to him. 'You might have rung or texted me.'

'I was ashamed,' he mutters.

'Is that an answer?'

Mum starts up.

'Zinny—'

'I'm talking to Dad.' I glower at him. 'You got that? I'm talking to you.'

He turns his eyes on me. They're not drunken eyes. I'd know it if they were. Not violent either. I'd know that too. But somehow they look worse than both those things. I don't know why. Maybe that's what shame looks like. I've never seen it in him before. Well, I have a bit, when he sobers up after a bad night and regrets what he's done a few hours earlier, but it never lasts, and he doesn't look like this either. Whatever this is, it's different.

'What did you get sacked for?' I say.

'Drinking and driving. Third warning.'

'Tosser.'

'I know.'

'So what were we living off? You had money in your wallet. I saw some of it.'

'I won it,' he says. 'Got lucky with a bet. Just enough to tide us over for a few weeks and make it look like I was still working. But it was running out when all this happened.'

Mum shakes her head.

'You should have told me about this.'

'You should have told me stuff too,' he says.

And she's the one who looks away this time.

'Mum,' I say, 'you got to tell me the truth. Did you know about that big package of counterfeit money in our house?'

She turns straight back to me.

'No, love, on my honour. Do you believe me?'

'Course I do.'

'Really? You promise?'

'Yeah.'

I do believe her. She's not lying. I think of Romeo, and his smarmy eyes.

'It was that guy,' I say. 'He must have gone up to the room at the top of the pub where they were keeping the big packs of money, and walked out with one of them. While you were cleaning the floor below.'

'I'm so sorry, Zinny,' she says.

I turn back to Dad. He's staring down at the floor now, his fists clenched.

'So where did you go during the daytime?' I say. 'Are you going to answer me this time or just belt me like you normally do?'

He doesn't move, doesn't speak.

'I started checking the milometer on your van,' I say, 'and you were clocking up way more than you should have been each day. So what was that about? Were you having a fling as well?'

'No,' he growls, and he shoots a glance at Mum.

'So what were you doing?'

'Looking for work,' he snaps, 'driving all over the city and then further afield, and all for nothing. That's what I was doing, Zinny, if you must know. Trying to get a bloody job. And coming home without one and wondering what the hell I'm going to say to you two when the money runs out.'

'Useless git,' I mutter.

Mum reaches out suddenly and strokes my head.

'He's not a useless git, Zinny.'

'He is.'

'He's not, Zinny, he's really not.'

I stare up at her. She's frowning and she looks close to tears again.

'He's your dad,' she says quietly, 'and he's no worse a parent than I am.'

'That's not saying much.'

'Was that a joke?'

She goes on watching me, and the frown's still there, and the tears below the surface, even though I can't see them.

'It was a joke,' I say.

She doesn't answer.

'Maybe not a very good one,' I add.

She glances round at Dad, then back at me.

'He did a brave thing too, Zinny.'

'Like what?'

'Made the driver of your car crash into the wall.'

'How come?'

'Didn't you see?'

'No,' I say. 'I was watching Flash Coat. He just raised the gun and everything went black.'

Mum glances at Dad again.

'Tell him,' she says.

He doesn't, just looks away.

'I will, then,' she says. 'Zinny, listen—'

'I don't want to.'

'Listen,' she says. 'You must, Zinny, because you're not being fair. Your dad was driving towards the railway bridge from the other side just as your car broke through. He saw you in the back with a gun pointed at your head and swung the van in front of the car. The driver swerved to avoid him and ploughed into the wall at the side of the road. So the policeman said. It was a brave thing to do, Zinny.'

I turn my eyes back on Dad. He shakes his head.

'It wasn't brave,' he says. 'It was reckless. I mean, if I'd only thought about it. You could have been killed crashing into that wall, and I'd have caused it. But everything happened so fast and I acted on instinct.'

'If you hadn't done it, Zinny would have been shot,' says Mum.

'It was still reckless,' says Dad.

The silence returns with that same heaviness, only this time it feels different. Not sure if it's better or worse. Dad takes a long, weary breath.

'But I did do one thing right,' he says.

He stares down at the floor again.

'I bloody did one thing right.'

He goes on, shuddering slightly.

'I know you're angry with me for disappearing, and I don't blame you, but the thing is . . . the reason I was gone all that time was . . . I've been driving and driving. You'll have a fit next time you check the milometer, Zinny, but listen, it was worth it because . . .'

He looks up again.

'I drove to Coniston, see?'

'What?' I say.

'It was that book with the nature photos that did it, the one you gave your mum. I just thought how much it meant to you, and then I saw your mum's face when she was looking at it, and that picture called Moon over Coniston, and I thought . . .'

He stares at us both, his eyes still dark and ashamed.

'I thought, is that place really as beautiful as it looks? And . . . how do people get to live somewhere like that? I mean . . . maybe there's work there, maybe there's a future for us there.'

'What have you done?' says Mum.

'I got a job working for a farmer in Coniston.'

'You what?'

But she heard him all right.

'You crazy man,' she says. 'You daft crazy man.'

'I told him about getting sacked,' he goes on, 'about

the drink and stuff. He says he'll take a punt on me. He's lost two men recently, he says, and he needs some help. Bit of driving, bit of fencing, bit of mucking in with this and that, whatever needs doing. He says I don't need the van because he's got all his own vehicles, so we can sell ours and pay off Mr Coily and still have something over for a small car. He's got work for you too, Dana, cleaning and helping out, and he says he'll train Zinny up in his school holidays if he's interested in farming. And Zinny, you could start running again. You'd love it up there.'

Dad looks at us hard, and for a moment the shame's gone from his face.

'We can do this,' he says. 'We can make a fresh start.'

The words sound strange. Maybe it's because Dad's never said them before, or I'm not really hearing them. Because I've got pictures forming in my head: of fields and fells, and the moon over a lake on a long, still night. A fresh start, yeah, why not? Mum's nodding already, and smiling too. But I just close my eyes.

And dream.

Tim Bowler is one of the UK's most compelling and original writers for teenagers. He was born in Leigh-on-Sea and after studying Swedish at university, he worked in forestry, the timber trade, teaching, and translating before becoming a full-time writer. He lives with his wife in a quiet Devon village and his workroom is a small wooden outhouse known to friends as 'Tim's Bolthole'.

Tim has written nineteen books and won fifteen awards, including the prestigious Carnegie Medal for *River Boy*, and his provocative *BLADE* series is being hailed as a groundbreaking work of fiction. He has been described by the *Sunday Telegraph* as 'the master of the psychological thriller' and by the *Independent* as 'one of the truly individual voices in British teenage fiction'.

www.timbowler.co.uk

1

SO HE'S LOOKING at me with his puggy face, this big jerk of a policeman, and I'm thinking, take him out or let him live?

Big question.

I don't like questions. Questions are about choices and choices are a pain. I like certainties. Got to do this, got to do that, no debate. Take him out, let him live. Know what you got to do. Certainty.

Only I'm not certain here. I'm pretty sure I want to take him out. I hate the sight of him and I hate being back at the police station.

The knife feels good hidden inside my sock. Pugface didn't even feel it when he frisked me. But he'll feel it pretty quick if he doesn't treat me right. It's only a small blade but I know how to use it.

He's still watching me with those pig-eyes.

'Right, young man,' he says.

'I'm not your young man.'

He takes no notice. He's too busy smirking.

'In your own words,' he goes on.

'In your own words what?'

'In your own words—what happened?'

'What happened where?'

He gives this heavy, exaggerated sigh. I hate that. Move my fingers slowly down my thigh.

He can't see with the desk in the way. That bosomy policewoman over by the door's watching but she can't see anything either. I can tell from her face.

Anyway, she's too far away. I can have my knife out and into Pugface before she's covered half the ground between us. Probably time to stick her too.

He goes on in that patronizing voice.

'What happened at the pedestrian crossing?'

My fingers are close to the knife now. I stop my hand. No need to move it any further. I'm safe enough. All that's needed is a lunge and a thrust. Maybe a bit more if Bosoms gets involved.

'What happened at the crossing?' says Pugface.

'Nothing.'

'You stood in the road after the lights had turned to green and refused to move and let the traffic pass.'

'Did I?'

'You shouted abuse at the drivers waiting to move on.'

'Can't remember.'

'Especially the man in the nearest car.'

'Can't remember.'

'The man in the green estate. He asked you to move aside so that he and everybody else could drive on. You swore back at him and made obscene gestures.'

'He was rude to me.'

'You don't think maybe you were the one being rude?'

I shrug. I'm starting to enjoy this now.

'Eh?' says Pugface.

'Don't know.'

'It was dangerous.'

'No, it wasn't. He was never going to run me over.'